Deception
in a Small Town

A Novel By
ANNE TARLETON

© 2011 Anne Tarleton
All Rights Reserved.

No part of this publication may be reproduced, stored in a retrieval system, or transmitted, in any form or by any means, electronic, mechanical, photocopying, recording, or otherwise, without the written permission of the author.

First published by Dog Ear Publishing
4010 W. 86th Street, Ste H
Indianapolis, IN 46268
www.dogearpublishing.net

ISBN: 978-145750-093-0

This book is printed on acid-free paper in the United States of America.

This is a work of fiction. Characters, locations, institutions, and organizations in this novel either are the product of the author's imagination or, if real, are used fictitiously without the intent to describe their actual conduct, except as noted below:

References in this novel to events or activities concerning United States Federal agencies and the American Cancer Society, along with the Brooks Trust as described by Dr. James Bennett and Dr. Thomas DiLorenzo in their book *Cancer Scam*, are true.

The author has made an effort to provide accurate Internet addresses at the time of publication. Neither the publisher nor the author assumes any responsibility for errors, or for changes that occur after publication.

Acknowledgement

I would like to thank Transaction Publishers of New Brunswick, New Jersey, for permission to use excerpts from Drs. Bennett and DiLorenzo's book, *Cancer Scam*.

Cancer Scam is a follow-up to Bennett and DiLorenzo's first book, *Unhealthy Charities: Hazardous to Your Health and Wealth;* a brave effort that brilliantly shows how government bureaucrats steal funds intended for the highest public purpose and use them for narrow political advancement.

I would also like to thank Mr. Bennett Weiner, COO of the Better Business Bureau for his kind permission to use excerpts from the BBB *Wise Giving Alliance* website.

Dedicated to Vicki

Deception
in a Small Town

"A large rose-tree stood near the entrance of the garden: the roses growing on it were white, but there were three gardeners at it, busily painting them red. Alice thought this a very curious thing, and she went nearer to watch them…"

—Lewis Carroll

Alice's Adventures in Wonderland

❧ Chapter One ☙

*A*lison slammed the hatch of her Jeep Cherokee. After six months of planning, the day had finally arrived. She stood alone in front of the home that she had known for nine years, five of them with Jack…so many memories. Dinah, her Doberman pinscher, was safely crated and ready to travel. According to Alison's travel plans, the road ahead led two thousand miles to a small town on the Western Slope of Colorado. Her plan was to average 300 miles each day. It was early April and she still could run into a spring storm across Missouri or Kansas, but her goal was to get to Rosemont, Colorado, before the moving truck arrived in ten days. As she entered Interstate 80 going west, her mind traveled back to the beginning with Jack.

They had met in 1991 as volunteers at a Habitat for Humanity remodel project in Newark, New Jersey. Jack was an idealist, and he was always ready to help his fellow man. She remembered how surprised she was when she learned he was a corporate lawyer. It seemed like a strange combination: an *altruistic lawyer*? Alison, like so many others, held the perception that lawyers were all opportunists. It was only after they started dating that she learned Jack had survived a failed marriage, which he admitted was his fault. That first marriage, during those years he was climbing the corporate ladder were frustrating for his wife at that time. He was not able to balance the personal and professional demands. He could not keep everyone happy. He had made his choices, the profession ones, mostly driven by youthful ambition. Years later, the volunteer work became his way of making up for his earlier years of selfishness and indifference. At the time Alison identified with that mindset, remembering how focused she was on her own work as an assistant product manager at Merck, the large pharmaceutical company. She wanted to be a part of finding cures to dread diseases and treatments for chronic disorders. In those days, work always came first, and if friends didn't understand it, she remembered she didn't much care.

Now, at the age of 50, she was leaving everything familiar to her. Alison was looking for a circle of new friends, a support system in a new town whom she could grow old with. Over the years, she had made excuses to her family for her absence at too many Christmas and Easter dinners, and then her family just stopped expecting her. In those early years, her coworkers at Merck knew her better than her own mother did. Her work was her life. She recognized that part in Jack when they first started dating.

She remembered when she met him how things changed…or perhaps she was ready for a change and Jack was her new purpose. Either way, it was meant to be, because they shared ten wonderful years together. She remembered they only dated for seven months, then married. At the time it seemed like a short courtship, and she was warned that whirlwind romances never worked out. But for the two of them—Jack, 42, and Alison, 35—they both knew they could make it work, even with Jack's personal history and her lack of it. There was no formality, no big church wedding. Her family was just glad she finally was getting married, and they didn't much care who it was to. Jack didn't have any family, except a half brother in upstate

New York. Alison thought back now, remembering how many big church weddings had just ended in divorce. She still would rather have had the ten years with Jack than ten big church weddings, and she knew in her heart that the same was true for Jack, too.

Driving down the interstate, Alison recalled the commute she had from Jack's apartment in Manhattan to Merck laboratories in New Jersey, and the many nights they had been apart due to her schedule at the lab. She remembered the many times she had stayed late for a meeting or when she was running an experiment. Cheryl, Alison's secretary at Merck, had been kind to share her apartment in Lawrenceville with her on those late nights or when the weather was bad. So, after four years of commuting, and too many nights apart, she and Jack decided to move out of the City. She recalled the many discussions they had, how they finally reached a compromise. That compromise was Rockaway, a small suburb halfway between Jack's work in the City and her work at Merck. When the small white clapboard-sided house came on the market, it seemed like destiny and they bought it. Alison remembered that day as if it was yesterday.

A light drizzle was hitting the windshield now as she grabbed for the tissue box on the passenger's seat.

"All those memories," she thought as she dabbed at her eyes. All of that happened in 1995. Now, 11 years later, driving down the interstate, she was thinking to herself how many things she wished she could have said to Jack before he died. She wished she had thanked him more, kissed him more, and laughed with him more. She remembered there were many families in New York and New Jersey who didn't have that opportunity to say good-bye on September eleventh, five years ago. Jack's office was on the fortieth floor in the North Tower of the World Trade Center; he died just three weeks before their tenth wedding anniversary. But you never know when sudden death will strike. Alison sometimes envied those families whose loved one lies dying in the hospital or at home with Hospice—those families with the opportunity to say good-bye.

The first year without Jack was the hardest. She tried to compensate with work but found the same old routine not enough to overcome the emptiness. She recalled it was also around this time that Merck was acquiring other pharmaceutical companies whose senior research staff would be jockeying for position within Merck. She couldn't deal with the petty bickering or infighting so common to mergers and takeovers. Perhaps it was that or just that she needed a new challenge, but it was a year after Jack's death that she changed jobs and went to work as a senior product manager for Cyclacel, a small biotechnology company in Short Hills, New Jersey that was closer to her home in Rockaway—and Dinah.

Jack and Alison always talked about getting a dog once they moved to the suburbs; they had so many plans. It was after a year of living alone that she decided to look for one, knowing Jack would want her to have a dog for company and protection. So the process of finding the right dog became Alison's quest, and one that was worth it.

At that moment, she heard Dinah turn in her crate and recalled the Saturday morning she went to a local dog show being held outside in one of the parks. The day was perfect. The air was still cool, but the sun was shining, and how good to get out of the house and not be going to work! Her day was spent studying at all the different dogs and investigating the dog handlers and owners with perhaps too many questions. That was her analytical mind; although appreciated in a scientific setting, it could sometimes, she had been told, be annoying to those around her. But she methodically had to consider all the advantages and disadvantages of each breed, and that took questions and answers to uncover. Most people were impatient with her, but she knew Jack always liked her mind.

Just then, Dinah stirred again in her travel crate and Alison realized they had been on the road for three hours. Spotting a rest stop up ahead, she pulled in off the interstate, just west of the Pocono Mountains. She opened the hatch then the door to the crate, put Dinah on her retractable leash, and the dog hopped out of the Jeep. She sniffed around, then, near a small patch of grass, she squatted and relieved herself. She looked back at Alison with eyes that spoke, "Thank you."

"I swear you could talk, just by looking at me," Alison thought to herself. They walked through the parking area, both stretching their legs, and Alison remembered the day Dinah found her. Not at the dog show—that day was just for questions and answers. But following a lead from the show, she had contacted a local Doberman breeder, who questioned Alison on her working hours. After hearing how many hours she spent away from home, he told Alison a puppy would not be suitable, as a puppy needs attention every three to four hours in order to be housebroken and fed. The breeder suggested an older dog and knew of a woman who couldn't keep an eight-month-old female Dobie. The following weekend, Alison went to see the dog. Dinah was in a crate in the woman's garage. When they went out into the garage and opened the crate, Dinah emerged, wagging her whole body that ended with a stubby cropped tail. She was very beautiful, coal black, and both ears stood straight up. Alison knelt down so the the dog could sniff her outstretched hand, then the dog put her head in Alison's lap.

Remembering that moment, Alison smiled. She had known then that this was *the* dog. And that Jack would have liked her, too. Alison later learned that Dinah would have been heading for a rescue program that found homes for older dogs; she was glad she found her before she went into the program.

Deception in a Small Town

When she was a child growing up, Alison's family never owned a dog, but her neighborhood was always full of them. Alison knew Dobermans were thought of as a vicious breed but she learned that it was only the lack of attention or teasing that made them so. Alison decided to enroll Dinah and herself in a basic dog classes at the local pet store. She recalled those first months. Dinah was initially shy, but congenial with the other dogs, and she was very patient with Alison, too. In those early training days, Alison tried to communicate what she wanted from Dinah, teaching her the basics of sit, stay, down, and come. Dinah wanted so much to please, but she sometimes didn't know what was being asked of her. Alison recalled learning that Dinah watched her body language and could read her every move. Her movements spoke to the dog. A bond formed between the two, along with trust on both their parts. Dinah trusted Alison to care for her, and Alison learned to trust Dinah's ability to read people and protect her. The more Alison worked with Dinah and learned about the breed, the more she was convinced that she had made a good decision. Doberman pinschers are loyal, protective, and very smart. ("Smarts" was a characteristic Alison respected.) Their short coat made them good indoor dogs, and their appearance with cropped ears and tail, while very intimidating, was nothing like their true temperament.

Dinah hopped back into the Jeep. Alison closed the hatch and they were soon back on the interstate.

The trip through Ohio and Indiana took two days, and after Alison reorganized the Jeep so she could more easily get to the overnight bag and Dinah's kibbles, the two traveling companions settled into a routine. This was not the first overnight trip she and Dinah had made together. One summer, she recalled taking her camping in the Catskills with a group from work, and Dinah did well. She didn't seem to mind the strange, cramped surroundings as long as she could put her head in Alison's lap or rest against her leg. Dinah never ran off, and Alison was grateful for that.

All the motels along the planned route to Colorado had been researched earlier, and only those that allowed pets were considered. They were usually located on the outskirts of the larger towns, such as Cleveland and Davenport. Alison usually found a small park near the town's Visitor Center to walk Dinah if she couldn't find a rest stop off the interstate. They ran into high winds and hail outside of Omaha but, fortunately, there was no snow. Alison was enjoying the freedom. "No commitments, no place to be, no meetings to attend—just me, Dinah, and 'on the road again,'" she sang along with Willie Nelson.

Just outside the Colorado state line, Alison turned onto Highway 76. The highway followed the South Platte River for miles. Often, cottonwood trees blocked the view of the river or the river pulled away from the highway and hid in arroyos below the uncultivated arid land. Alison thought about the first pioneers who traveled this same route a hundred years ago.

As the river braided its way south, it again turned away from the road towards the dirt cliffs to the north. The land between the winding river and the arrow-straight road was now flat and full of plowed fields where rows of spring corn and wheat would be fed by the river all summer long. "This is real farming country," Alison thought to herself, "just beautiful." She arrived in Fort Morgan, Colorado, on schedule. It had been one of those towns she considered for her relocation; with a population of around 27,000, it was the size she was looking for, but it was so flat, like New Jersey, and Alison was determined to live near mountains.

Deception in a Small Town

She remembered reading a little of Fort Morgan's history during her search for a small Midwest town. She recalled reading that Fort Morgan was built to protect the mail service and immigrants along the Overland Trail, and it was known as the "Fort Morgan Cut Off" for the Overland Trail. The town was built at the point where the trail left the South Platte River and headed across the plains directly towards Denver.

Alison turned off at the exit to the motel she had booked. The middle-aged woman sitting behind the front desk seemed pleasantly indifferent. Greeting her, she peered over Alison's shoulder to get a glimpse of her car. "She's probably checking out my license plates," Alison thought. That had happened a lot on this trip, and Alison couldn't wait to get Colorado tags on her Jeep. Alison took the key from the woman and offered a smile. "Oh, is there a park where I can walk my dog?" she asked the woman.

"Sure," the woman said, "try Riverside Park, just off the highway on the north side. You can't miss it."

"Thanks," Alison replied.

Once she had unloaded those things she and Dinah would need for the one-night stay, she got back in the car to go looking for Riverside Park. The woman at the motel was right, it was easy to find. Alison pulled into the parking lot, put Dinah on her leash, and started walking. The park was beautiful. It had two well-maintained baseball fields, and picnic areas were scattered in clusters on the still-brown lawns. She could imagine this park on a Sunday afternoon in the summertime, full of families playing ball and barbequing. She and Dinah walked over to the duck pond that was located in the center of the park. The Canada geese were everywhere on the pond, resting on their journey north. Dinah got excited when a few of them flew away, honking and squawking their warning. Alison spotted a brass plaque set into a stone pedestal at one end of the park and headed in that direction. Once there, she read the words inscribed:

Fort Morgan exemplified the pioneer spirit of the times and its progress and determination were noticed by those areas around it. This plaque is in commemoration of Republican President Theodore Roosevelt who in 1905 stopped his train in Fort Morgan and gave a short speech to over 1000 people gathered at the train station. He praised the hard work and industry of the residents toward the reclamation of the Great Plains into viable farmland.

"How nice," Alison thought, "to remember these moments in a town's history." One more walk around the duck pond and Alison headed back to the motel. It had been a long day.

The next morning Alison loaded the Jeep and drove back to the park for a short walk with Dinah, then back in the Jeep. The morning sky was clear as Alison entered the highway. It was going to be a good day. Once out of Fort Morgan, it was only fifty miles to the outskirts of Denver, Colorado. With the sun behind her, she continued to drive west. She could see the magnificent Rocky Mountains rising up from the flatlands of the plains. From Denver, she would pick up Interstate 70 and drive west through the mountains. The weather was going to be clear for the next three days, and Alison was looking forward to going through the historic towns of Georgetown, Frisco, and Glenwood Springs. She had read about the construction of the famous Eisenhower Tunnel and had seen photos of the highway through Glenwood Canyon. At the top of Vail Pass, she would be at ten thousand feet. Alison set her camera on the passenger seat, along with her bottled water and Kleenex. "It's going to be a good day, right Dinah?" Alison said over her shoulder.

❧ Chapter Two ☙

By the time she entered Denver proper, the morning commuter rush was over and the roads were dominated by speeding delivery trucks and large semi-trailers. The climb out of Denver towards Idaho Springs was slow, but it didn't matter to Alison: She was enjoying the drive. She stopped along the river to rest and give Dinah a potty break. The cold air smelled of pines trees and diesel exhaust.

Back on the road, Eisenhower Tunnel came up sooner than Alison had anticipated. She pulled over to take a picture, then got back in the car and drove on to Frisco. The drive took Alison past Dillon Reservoir and Copper Mountain Ski Area, where there was still dust-covered snow on some of the ski runs and drifts on the north-facing slopes. The Jeep started to gain altitude as the four-lane highway neared Vail Pass, a climb to 10,603 feet. Many of the large trucks and semi-trailers were passing her, but Alison didn't care—it gave her more time to take in the views.

At the top of Vail Pass, Alison took the exit and turned into the Visitor Center. She parked in the lot, with the intention of taking Dinah out for a short hike in the area. The air was thin and just the short walk up the steps to the center winded her, but Dinah didn't seem bothered. They wandered around the perimeter of the building, Dinah finding all sorts of interesting smells to investigate and Alison slowly following, taking in all the beauty and nature around her. The two friends wandered for a full half-hour until Alison, realizing the time that had passed, started coaxing Dinah back in the direction of the Jeep.

Once back on the interstate, the downgrade into Vail Valley caused Alison to downshift to slow the engine, "I'll make a mountain driver yet," she said to herself.

Alison was now looking forward to the 16-mile-long drive through Glenwood Canyon, which cradles the Colorado River between the towns of Glenwood Springs and Gypsum. She remembered reading that this section of the interstate started in the 1980s. It was a huge undertaking and engineering challenge. Alison recalled reading that the main reason the construction work disturbed so little of the canyon was because of a method never before used in the United States. Known as "balanced cantilever" construction, the method works by building a bridge from above rather than below. A bridge column was first built, and then a special crane known as a "gantry" is positioned atop the column. The gantry builds the bridge outward from the column using pre-cast segments that are trucked in to the site.

One of the biggest problems during the construction of the interstate had been that there was no traffic control coordination, which Alison thought must surely have added to the confusion and safety issues during that time. Until coordination between contractors was consolidated under a single authority, she recalled reading, the delays in the canyon were dangerous and unsafe. Once the traffic management program coordinated traffic using hand radios and flaggers, the public traffic could be led through the canyon with pilot cars. The program was successful and, on a good day, the traffic had proceeded with only a single stop in the canyon of thirty minutes; on a bad day, she could only imagine.

❧ Chapter Three ❧

In Rifle, Colorado, she found the hotel on the other side of the highway. Once settled in her room, she made a phone call to her real estate agent, Ron Hayes, in Rosemont. She told him she would be arriving tomorrow around ten in the morning and that she would stop by the office to pick up the keys to the house

Alison remembered how she had found Ron, and she felt very lucky he had been willing to work with her. Six months earlier, Alison had reviewed Rosemont's real estate home listings online; she signed onto three real estate websites and told each of them what she was looking for. Ron had been the first to contact her and introduce himself. Alison had told him her situation and time frame, then asked if he could work with her long distance. He was very willing to accommodate her needs. Ron had three other agents in his small office and over the past six months, she had gotten to know them all by phone or email. She now considered them her first friends in Rosemont. After viewing homes on the internet, and sending Ron out to look at them, they finally found exactly what Alison was looking for and at the right price. They sent photos of every room, window, and closet in the house, the front and backyards, as well as the inside of the detached garage; Ron even sent e-mail photos of the house next door, the streets with snow on them, and the sidewalk out front by the parkway. Ron spoke to the neighbors and listened to traffic during the 5 o'clock rush hour. Ron was her eyes and ears: He made the purchase of this 1930s-built home remarkably easy for her, instead of the dubious endeavor that most of Alison's coworkers had warned her it would be. She knew most of the skeptics had never ventured out of New Jersey, so one must always consider the source. She pulled up to the real estate office on Town Street and left the car running so Dinah could have air. It was cool outside, but the sun could still warm the car quite quickly. She would only be a moment. Ron was there to greet her with a big smile and enthusiastic handshake. He was easy to recognize from the Christmas card his office sent out to clients for the holidays—a tall man with a full head of brown curly hair. He wore a nice pair of dress jeans and cowboy boots.

"Hi, I'm Ron. How'd the trip go?" he asked as his hand went out to shake hers.

"Fine, thank you," Alison replied with a smile, putting her hand out in return. "I have my dog in the car out front. May I have the key so I can go unload her and my luggage? Is there anything else I need to sign?" she asked, somewhat impatiently. "Sorry, but I'm anxious to see the house."

"Sure, no problem. Here's the key...," Ron said. "I'll be just behind you after I finish up with these clients. Joyce here will draw you directions to the house."

"Thanks, see you soon," Alison smiled, taking the house key. Joyce, the office receptionist, drew a small map with directions to the house and handed it to her.

"Thanks, Joyce," she said as she headed out the door. The address was 1203 Hartford Avenue, four blocks from the library in a well-maintained, established neighborhood south of the town center. As Alison turned down Hartford Avenue, she recognized the house immediately. She drove into the driveway, thinking it was prettier than any of the pictures Ron had sent. It felt like she was coming home. After six months of planning and many sleepless nights, she was finally here.

She got out and went around back to let Dinah out of her crate. Clipping on her leash, she took the dog around to the backyard. Recalling the locations of the gates from the photographs Ron had sent, Alison checked them all to make sure they were closed, then she let Dinah off her leash. The Dobie hurriedly sniffed, then ran back to Alison as if to say, "Guess what I just learned!" Then she was off again, sniffing here and there, then ran back again as if to say, "Can we stay?"

"Yes Dinah, we can stay." Alison never grew tired or impatient with her dog's energy. It was her enthusiasm for discovery that Alison enjoyed watching so much. As she watched Dinah play in her new backyard, Ron came walking through the gate. Dinah, alert to an intruder, started barking, and Ron stopped dead in his tracks.

"She's quite a guard dog," Ron said. "I forgot about her," he added. Alison told Dinah, "Quiet…sit," then walked over to Ron and shook his hand while the Dobie watched the exchange. Alison called Dinah over. She came and sat between Alison and Ron, and Alison told Ron to hold out a closed fist for her to sniff. He did, and once the introduction was over, Dinah was fine.

"Thanks for your patience," she said. "Let's go inside." On the way across the concrete patio, Ron asked, "When is the furniture arriving?"

"Tomorrow," she said. "I can't thank you enough for all your help. You and your staff did a great job. When I get unpacked and settled, I would love to have you and your wife over for dinner," she told him.

"That would be nice," Ron said. "Will you need any help tomorrow?" he asked.

"Thanks…if that was an offer," she smiled, embarrassed, thinking that she might have been presumptuous. "But the movers will be here pretty much all day, placing the furniture and separating boxes," she said.

"Well," Ron said, "the electricity and gas were turned on yesterday, so you should have lights and hot water tonight. You'll have to call for phone and cable hookup. Do you have a cell phone?"

"Yes, of course," she replied with a smile. Alison was getting tired, she needed a break and Ron seemed to see it on her face.

"Let me know if you need anything else. My son has a soccer game tonight, but I'll be on my cell. You have that number?"

"Yes, I do."

"Welcome to Rosemont," Ron smiled, then went out the front door. Standing alone in the small entry of her new house, with Dinah happily exploring in the new yard, Alison felt content for the first time in years.

Chapter Four

Alison unloaded her overnight bag, the sleeping bag, and Dinah's crate from the Jeep. She decided to "nest" in the alcove off the main room until the furniture arrived tomorrow. The house was not yet a home, but eventually—with her things around and pictures on the wall—it would come to life, reflecting her hopes for a new life. This bungalow-style house was built in the traditional style of the 1930s. Ron told her there had been a major remodeling done in the early '80s when wiring, plumbing, and gas lines had been brought up to code. The old windows were replaced with double pane four-paneled sliders and the exterior doors were changed over to meet fire codes. Ron had found a set of the remodel plans and sent them to Alison when she showed serious interest in the house. She had learned so much about construction and remodeling during those years with Jack as a volunteer work for Habitat for Humanity. Reading a set of blueprints was no problem. When she first received the plans she noticed that a space that was originally part of the entry had been given up to accommodate a set of very steep, narrow stairs, built to access the second floor. The living space on the second story was created by converting the large attic, directly over the kitchen, living, and dining room areas, to a master suite, which had a large bedroom and bath.

Deception in a Small Town

The ceiling and walls over the new living space were insulated with R35—more than code required, but because heat rises, it added to the thermal efficiency on a cold snowy night when the temperature dipped below zero. Alison planned to make this the master bedroom. Away from the work that happened in the rest of the house, it would be her oasis, where she could feel safe and watch the stars at night through the west-facing dormer window.

The floor of the master bath was finished with white tiles that ran halfway up the walls, giving them a wainscot look. She didn't mind the antiseptic look of white tile everywhere, because it allowed her to use any color towels or wall coverings she wanted, and the room would still look very nice. The enclosed shower was also tiled in white, but they were smaller, and she liked the interest created by their different size. All the fixtures were white porcelain, so the space was very bright, but she knew she could easily tone it down with different-colored accessories. A small window was installed at the time of the remodel, which created the natural ventilation required by code, while at the same time offering a hint of morning light. The bathroom plumbing was stacked over the kitchen area to make efficient use of the hot and cold running water, as well as providing sewer access for the toilet. The opposite wall of the suite had built-in storage, which was so useful for linens and towels. Alison remembered this feature from Ron's description, recalling her thoughts on the functional benefits designed into this area of the house. Overall, she thought it was a well-planned remodel. She could tell that the contractor focused on function and safety rather than facades or finishes. As the new owner of this home, she appreciated his priorities.

As she came down the stairs, Alison thought about what color to eventually paint the master bedroom—perhaps a moss green with white accents. Then, turning right, she entered the kitchen. Ron had sent pictures of the appliances, so Alison could decide if she wanted them replaced. They were only a few years old and all in good working order. Alison had told Ron she would keep them all. The kitchen was L-shaped with ten-foot ceilings. The sink was under the south-facing window, which overlooked the front porch and faced Hartford Avenue. Even though it was south-facing, the roof overhang shaded the porch from most of the summer sun, but still let in enough light during the day. Alison remembered reading, during her research on house design, how traditional it was to have the sink under the window, and there were many theories why this design remains so popular. "More than likely, the traditional design came from the need to pass food from the garden in to the preparation area, as well as having natural light to work by; then there was the ease of tossing refuse outside…pre-plumbing days," Alison thought out loud. "Or perhaps the tradition started when women still washed dishes in the sink, before the dishwasher or throw-away styrofoam plates," she thought. "Looking out the window would be a pleasant distraction while working at the sink. Today, there are iPods, CDs, and tapes plugged into our ears…it doesn't really matter what people are looking at anymore," she thought to herself. Standing at the sink, she noticed the National Kitchen and Bath's recommended three-foot counter used as a workspace next to the sink. She liked that. The gas stove was on an outside wall, and she was pleased when she learned it was vented out, rather than having a circulating fan. Then the counter turned and the refrigerator was placed at the end of that run. The pantry, or built-in storage, ran along the opposite wall. The pleated doors were divided into sections and opened on the top and bottom, allowing the clearance needed for the four-place breakfast table that was planned for the center of the kitchen. The shelving was deep enough to accommodate large iron skillets and bulky items, like

Deception in a Small Town

Dinah's food and dog biscuits. She really liked that feature and thought how great it would have been to have that in her lab back in New Jersey—but this wasn't New Jersey. Then she wondered what time it was back there. She thought about calling Bill, back at the lab, to tell him she made it okay. He would be the one to worry. Bill was always looking for the down side of any situation, and Alison fondly remembered labeling him her pessimist. But oftentimes, his pessimism saved the company thousands of research dollars and hours of laboratory time. He had the ability to see pitfalls within a protocol's methodology that the others couldn't see until the project was well underway. Alison remembered the many lengthy discussions with Bill, and she knew she would miss that intellectual volleying. "It's probably too late to call him now…I'll call tomorrow," she thought.

  The other end of the kitchen opened into the dining room through a passage supported by an exposed lintel. The dining room was in the northwest corner of the house and had windows on two walls. One set of windows offered the view north into the backyard and the other set opened west onto the side of the yard and the garage. With the built-in hutch on the opposite wall, there was little wall space for oil paintings. But storage for china was more important to Alison than wall space, anyway. After all her research on home design, this was really the house she would build for herself, if she ever had the notion. There were so many thoughtful functional details. The dining room joined the living or main room on the north side of the house. There was a window at each corner of the north living room wall, offering views of the backyard. On the wall between those two windows, Alison envisioned her collection of photographs and etchings arranged nicely in groups of three. Opposite that wall, toward the center of the house, was the brick fireplace with a raised hearth, which faced into the living area. The back of the fireplace created the separation between the hallway and the living area. One could walk behind the brick fireplace to the hallway and then back to the stairs at the entry leading to the second floor. "You never feel boxed in anywhere in the house," Alison thought. The space throughout the house felt open, yet the rooms themselves were very cozy, the way a traditional bungalow design was supposed to be. There were glass-paneled doors at the end of the hall leading to the side porch, which connected to the front porch. She liked these glass-paneled doors because they added light to the east corner of the house, but she knew they would have to be covered for privacy. Perhaps a sheer material, she thought to herself.

Off in the opposite corner of the living room was the small 8 by 12-foot enclosed alcove. This was where Alison had placed her sleeping bag and overnight things. The double doors could be left open, adding space to the adjoining living room, or the doors could be closed and the alcove could serve as a guest room or private office. Alison hadn't decided. The alcove had one small window on the same wall as the glass-paneled double doors, adding light and fresh air to the small space.

There was a scratching sound on the double doors and Alison saw Dinah waiting there to come in. She was such good company. Letting her into the room, Alison arranged Dinah's blanket next to her own sleeping bag on the floor of the alcove then went to the kitchen with Dinah at her heels and started fixing the dog's kibbles.

"Sorry, no scrapings from the table tonight, pretty girl," Alison told her. "I'll go shopping tomorrow." Dinah knew the word "tomorrow" meant that something special was going to happen. She could pick out key words from full sentences and know exactly what to expect. If Alison was on the phone and used the word "walk," Dinah would go into an acrobatic dance that wouldn't stop until Alison hung up the phone. Alison had to start spelling words out instead of saying them, and when she did, her friends would tell her, "Say hi to Dinah," knowing the dog was close by.

When Alison first got Dinah, she used to sing the words to the song, "Tomorrow," from the theatre production of *Annie*. Jack had taken Alison to see the play on the New York stage for their anniversary; that was the year before he was killed. So now, the song and the story had special meaning to Alison, and that in turn gave it special meaning for Dinah, too. "Yes, Dinah, tomorrow, tomorrow, I love ya tomorrow, you're only a day away..." Alison sang out, and Dinah jumped and barked, sharing in the song's optimism.

As Dinah ate her kibbles, Alison dug out a bag of cookies and a bottle of water for herself. Tomorrow would come soon.

ॐ Chapter Five ॐ

Her cell phone rang at 8 a.m. The movers were in town having breakfast and wanted directions to the house. Alison found the instructions she had gotten from Ron's office and read them to the driver. They would be here in about 30 minutes, right after their breakfast. Alison rushed to get Dinah fed and put her in the backyard, then she moved the dog's crate to the backyard, too. While the movers were here, Alison didn't want to take the chance of Dinah getting loose. People can be unintentionally careless, and Alison didn't want to offer any opportunities for carelessness. The plan was to keep Dinah in her crate under the shade of the big tree in the backyard until the truck pulled away and all the gates and doors were checked. The Dobie would feel safe in her crate and Alison would be able to keep an on eye on her from the house.

Grabbing a hand towel and her toothbrush from her overnight bag, Alison went into the half-bath off the laundry room to clean up. Looking in the mirror over the small sink, she saw the reflection of a woman who had just turned 50 whose shoulder-length hair was now almost all gray. Her hazel eyes, slightly red from lack of a good night sleep, looked sunken in her pale lined complexion. Over the years, Alison had kept in shape and didn't look her age, and she could still probably pass for 45. She was very unassuming and could blend into a crowd well; no one ever considered her striking or beautiful, but "wholesome" was a word she once heard someone use to describe her. Today, in her new home, she liked being described that way.

What did make Alison unique was her self-confidence, and she had promised herself to keep that quality low keyed in her new community. She had learned that outside the science community, that trait was considered annoying, and that was not the first impression she wanted to make on her new town.

Dinah was learning that she got Alison to come when she scratched on the back door. Alison let the dog in, saying, "Yes, yes, Dinah. I will look into having a doggie door installed for you...and me," she smiled. Alison put Dinah on the leash, grabbed her purse, and went out the front door to the Jeep. She had to get some breakfast before the movers came. It was going to be a long day. She remembered passing a McDonalds off Main Street. Once on Main, she easily found the drive-through and ordered breakfast, promising herself to eat better once things settled down. Dinah loved the smell of Sausage McMuffins and always received the last bite of Alison's meal.

Alison drove up to the house just as the moving truck arrived. She parked across the street, grabbed her purse, breakfast bag, and the end of Dinah's leash, and rushed over to meet them. A man with a clipboard came over and said, "Hi, are you Mrs. Hansen? Nice dog," he added.

"Yes, please call me Alison," was her reply.

"Sure," the man said rather indifferently. "Can we back into the driveway?"

"I don't know if you can, but you may try, if you wish," she replied. She turned and walked Dinah into the backyard and put her in the dog crate all the while thinking to herself, "Now, Alison, don't confuse him with semantics, he just may drop something if he gets annoyed." Taking a bite of her breakfast, she went into the house and found the man carrying the clipboard, and said, "Sorry...where were we?" He was doing a walk-through, checking the width of the doorways into each room. Alison had methodically labeled each box with the room it was to go into, so the only decision was where the big pieces of furniture would be placed.

On one of her trips to the backyard to check on Dinah, Alison noticed a neighbor outside watering the lawn in the adjoining backyard. Alison waved and the neighbor waved back. "That's nice," Alison thought to herself, "very neighborly." The movers were very efficient. By 1 p.m., they had all the packing blankets folded up and put back into the moving truck. Alison, thanking them for all their good work, signed the manifest sheet on the man's clipboard, took the copy he handed her, then went inside. She was alone again, but now at least she had all her material memories around her, waiting to be released from their styrofoam and bubble-wrap bondage. She let Dinah out of her crate, and the dog joined Alison in the living room. Even through the plastic wrap and cardboard boxes, Dinah recognized the scents of familiar things as she moved from box to box. The Dobie seemed to say, "These smells are familiar...I know this...and this, too! My furniture was worth the wait outside all day. I know where I am...I'm home!"

The next few days were spent unpacking. It had been weeks since Alison had seen many of these treasures she had so carefully packed back in New Jersey, and it seemed like Christmas, opening each of the boxes and unwrapping dishes and crystal glasses. The cable TV and landline telephone were hooked up, and Alison connected the entertainment system without a problem, having taken photos of the wiring system prior to unhooking it. "Just follow the enclosed diagram," she said to herself. She had learned that trick from an experienced technician at Merck laboratory, who always took photos of equipment before it was moved or parts changed out. "Just thinking ahead," she remembered he always said.

❧ Chapter Six ❧

One morning after walking Dinah around the block, Alison was out in the yard cleaning up after the dog and deciding whether to plant a garden or make the interior of the house her first priority, when she heard someone call out, "Hi, neighbor!" It was the woman Alison had seen in the adjoining yard; her face was shaded under a sunhat and she was watering her lawn.

"Hi there," Alison hollered back. Both women went to the half fence separating the two yards, Dinah joining Alison. As Dinah came up, the woman stepped back. "Oh, she's okay with people…as long as I'm okay," Alison reassured her.

"Hi, my name is Connie," said the woman.

"Nice to meet you, Connie. My name is Alison, and this is Dinah."

"Ron told me when the house was sold, that a single woman was moving in," she continued.

"Oh, you know Ron?" Alison asked.

Connie chuckled. "Alison, this is a small town—information doesn't have to be on the front page of the *Rosemont Press* to be considered newsworthy! Yes, I know Ron, and the whole family for that matter. I taught his second son in middle school."

"Oh, so you're a teacher?" Alison asked.

"Retired now. I do substitute if someone gets sick. So, you're single…divorced?" Connie asked probingly.

As Alison watched Connie holding the garden hose, she thought she might as well tell this woman enough to water down her curiosity. She just didn't know if Connie was someone she wanted to take into her confidence. Being cautious, she decided to tell her only what she didn't mind seeing on the second page of the local newspaper.

"Widowed. My husband, Jack, died five years ago this coming September eleventh," Alison said, assuming Ron had also told Connie she had moved from New Jersey. Knowing the national news media had focused on the fact that many of the families who lost loved ones had lived in New Jersey, she waited to see how astute Connie was with the information. There was a pause…and then Alison saw the light go on in Connie's mind.

"Oh, I am so sorry… Was he in one of the Twin Towers that was attacked?" Connie asked.

"Yes," Alison said, staring right into the eyes staring back at her. Alison sensed that Connie's reaction was honest and not contrived.

Back on the East Coast, most people knew someone who had died that day, but out here in Colorado, people didn't know how to respond. Changing the subject, Connie asked, "Will you be looking for work?"

"No, not right away," Alison replied.

"How do you feel about being a volunteer?" she asked, adding, "It's a great way to meet members of the community."

"I was a volunteer for Habitat for Humanity," Alison said.

"Well, why don't you join me tomorrow? I have a committee meeting and we're always looking for volunteers."

"Is it a local organization?" Alison asked.

"Well, *our* group is local, if that's what you mean," Connie responded. That's not what Alison meant, but rather than be annoying with too many questions, she decided to go and see for herself. Besides, her plans did include some volunteer time, so this seemed like a nice invitation. As the two women leaned against the picket fence in the shade of large cottonwood trees, they continued to share personal information.

At that moment, Alison felt she had entered a scene. A scene perhaps painted by Norman Rockwell of two women chatting together over a shared white fence in a backyard some where in a small farming town…and she was one of the women.

Chapter Seven

The next afternoon, Alison walked over to Connie's house and knocked on her screen door.

"So glad you decided to come," said Connie as she pushed open the squeaky door. Alison went in to find five other women sitting around a table, all chattering as if they hadn't seen each other in years. She heard at least three conversations going at the same time and wondered who was doing the listening. "I guess, as the newcomer, it's my role to listen," Alison thought to herself. They all looked to be in their late forties or early fifties, well groomed yet very casual, wearing polyester tops and slacks. Alison had to remember that this wasn't a company meeting at a large corporation, but a group whose purpose she had yet to learn. Connie introduced Alison to them.

"Ladies! Ladies! Please listen up. This is Alison, and she is new in Rosemont. She just moved into the old Andersen house. She's from out of state…please don't hold that against her because she wants to volunteer."

"Welcome, to Rosemont, Alison," a couple of the women said, half annoyed by the interruption, then they went back to their conversations. "Sit here next to me, Alison," Connie said.

"Thanks," Alison replied with a half smile. Sitting down, she nodded to the other women.

Deception in a Small Town

"So, Alison, Connie told us you just moved to Rosemont...where from?"

"Rockaway, New Jers—" Alison started to say, but before she could finish her sentence, one of the women interrupted saying, "Well, I'm fourth generation Hartmans, here in town."

"Oh, Marge, stop bragging just because the rest of us are only third generation," said one of the women, and continued on, saying, "You'll have to excuse Marge, Alison. Most of our families came here to farm in the thirties or after the war...and the families just stayed. We know everyone in town."

"...and for one hundred miles around," added Sally, who was sitting next to Alison. That remark brought chuckling from the other women. "Marge's family was one of the first to homestead in the area, and she never lets us forget that."

"What does that make me," Alison thought to herself, "being in *their* town for just two weeks? Perhaps I'm a weed in their homegrown garden of cultivated locals?" But Alison chose to say nothing; she didn't want to offend them, and it was true she wasn't a local. It was hard enough for anyone to move to a new town, to make new friends, and to feel welcome. These women would probably never know what it was like to be an "outsider," nor would they ever have the courage to move somewhere else. "Big fish-little pond sort of thing," Alison thought to herself. "Oh, well."

She knew there were trade-offs: It was between living all your life in one place where you knew your neighbors versus the advantages of enjoying other parts of the country, appreciating the food and festivals of other regions as she and Jack had done. Alison knew that, statistically, the older one gets, the harder it is to make job changes or move from a home, or even buy a new car. That's why, when she turned 50, she felt she had to think seriously about setting out a plan if she was going to move. The emotional and mental energy it took for her to decide on this move was enormous, and when the idea started distracting her from her work, she knew she had to make a decision. When the idea of relocating started to consume her thoughts even at the lab, she knew the move had become more important than her work, and she was too disciplined to ever compromise her work. So, she gave up her life's work and committed herself to her dream of moving to a small town. By choosing Rosemont over others towns, she hoped her leap of faith was wisely made. But at that moment, surrounded by these five clucking hens, Alison had a hard time clinging to that thought. While probably not their intention, she was feeling very isolated in the middle of these women.

"Shall we get started?" interrupted Connie, as she came back to the table with coffee and homemade cookies. It was then that Alison learned these women were committee chairs for this year's fundraising event for the National Cancer Association.

"Ladies, as the event chair again this year, I would like to know the status of each committee regarding volunteer recruitment. We have entertainment, food, media…and Bert, who's not here today, said he would run the lights at the high school again this year. So how many teams do we have signed up? Marge, you're in charge of that."

"We have five from last year, and three more from local small businesses who said they would check their employees to get a team together; the hospital is short-handed and some of the staff are on double shifts, so I don't think they will be very active this year," Marge continued.

"The Recruitment Rally is next week, how is that going?" Connie asked.

Over the next hour and a half, Alison listened to reports from the chairs of the food committee, the entertainment committee, the media committee, the logistics committee, and the finance committee. There were two other committees not represented at this meeting, and that fact seemed to concern Connie who, Alison learned, had the responsibility of explaining the progress of the fundraising efforts to the local National Cancer Association's representative. Rather than ask the million questions swirling in her head, Alison decided to wait and ask Connie at her next opportunity.

In front of each committee's chairperson was a high-gloss multicolored guidebook, which appeared to be specific to her committee. Sally, who was sitting on the other side of Alison, saw her eyeing her guidebook, so she offered it to Alison with a smile.

"Thanks," Alison said. She noticed with surprise the high-quality printing used to publish the guidebook. As a product manager with her biotechnology company, Cyclacel, Alison had spent many hours with advertising agencies in New York, and she knew these printed pieces were expensive to produce; she wondered who did their publishing—if it was done here in the States or farmed out overseas. So much of it was being done out of the country due to labor union-dictated wages here at home.

Opening the media guidebook, Alison saw the organization's mission statement printed on the inside cover. It read, "A community-based voluntary organization dedicated to reducing the extent of cancer as a health problem and the suffering it causes, through research, education and service."

Alison knew from her work with other nonprofit organizations that each one classified as 501-C3 must submit a mission statement when filing for nonprofit status. This way, if funds are spent for purposes other than those set out in the organization's mission statement, their tax-exempt status can be revoked. The mission statement defines the purpose of the tax-exempt company. And yes, it *is* a company, with all the legal protection awarded to any corporation. Alison had never realized how ambitious some mission statements could be, and this one was right up there on top as the most ambitious of all.

Turning the pages of Sally's media guidebook, Alison read the step-by-step outline of the method for publicizing the event. There was a list of who to contact, what to write, how to print it, and a timeline to pace the committee's progress. There were four-color illustrations inside the guidebook, which included generic articles that the National Cancer Association had preapproved for use in local newspapers, on radio stations, and as public service announcements. There were headings for "Best Practices" and "Rules of Conduct."

Leaning towards Sally, Alison whispered, "Do you follow all these requirements and meet all the criteria?"

"No," Sally said under her breath, "we're a small community…we don't even have a local radio station." Reading the confused look on Alison's face, Sally said, "Dear dear, you *do* look confused. You see, Alison, Danville, the next town over, is the closest town with a broadcasting radio station. Their broadcast covers all of Rosemont and the surrounding areas." Sally sat back like that explained it all, then, looking over at Alison and seeing the confused look still on her face, she added with a patronizing tone, "Oh, I forgot…how would you know any of this? You're a newcomer."

"Yes, I am new," said Alison, "and I'll need more background to understand. However, I *do* understand that if the radio station gets advertising dollars from some of the businesses in Rosemont, it should support the town's event…right?"

"Yes, but you see, last year, Danville had their own NCA fundraiser, because the National Cancer Association also wanted an event in that community. Last year was their first. Before that, Danville always participated in ours here in Rosemont. We got a lot of good hardworking volunteers from Danville, and it was good for both communities."

Deception in a Small Town

"But why did the NCA want to start another event?" asked Alison. "Seems like it doubles the cost of overhead expenses."

"I don't know that anyone ever asked," Sally said. "Oh, but it has caused quite a stir...it became a big disagreement among the volunteers."

"How so?" Alison whispered.

"At first, the volunteers from Danville told the NCA they didn't want to organize their own event, that they liked working with us here in Rosemont. There were a lot of families in Danville who had relatives here in Rosemont, and everyone enjoyed getting together for the fundraising event...it was fun for everyone. Well, the National Cancer Association kept pushing for an event in Danville, and the discussion ended up on the agenda of the Danville city council meeting. I heard that was one of the most crowded council meetings ever held. Administrators from the hospital, local business owners, and even the regional executive director from the NCA showed up for the meeting—who's not even with the NCA anymore."

"Who isn't?" Alison asked.

"...that regional executive director person with the NCA," Sally said with frustration.

"Oh, I'm sorry," Alison said.

"That's okay," Sally replied. "No one stays employed with the NCA very long," she added.

"Why?" asked Alison.

"I don't know," Sally said. "You ask silly questions," she added, looking at Alison suspiciously.

"I'm sorry," Alison said. "I don't know what is important and what isn't important...I'm new," she said, hoping it would soothe Sally's frustration. "Please go on..."

Accepting Alison's invitation, Sally continued. "Well, after that city council meeting, the council voted to have a separate NCA event in Danville. I remember at the time it was rumored that the hospital administrators in Danville were promised special services from the NCA if they pushed through the vote for a separate fundraising event."

"What services?" Alison asked.

"I don't really know. This is Rosemont's fourth year raising money for the NCA, and I don't know that we have seen any services from NCA," Sally whispered. "The newspaper from Danville reported the hospital's vote was due to the fact that so many of Danville's hospital employees had relatives or friends who have had cancer of one kind or another, and I heard that those who resisted the Danville event and wanted to continue participating in Rosemont were accused of not having any community spirit," she continued.

"So now, instead of a cooperative effort between two rural towns to raise funds for a common cause, there is resentment and competition between the two towns," Alison said.

"Yup, that just about sums it up. So that's why their radio station doesn't really like to publicize our fundraiser." Sally paused to sip her coffee. "They think that promoting our event will hurt their fundraising efforts in Danville, since Danville has their event two weeks after ours here in Rosemont."

"Really…I had no idea. That's a shame—the cooperation was lost," Alison said.

Alison thought the whole thing sounded absurd. Have these people lost sight of the purpose? Wasn't the whole point of the event about coming together and raising money for—what did their mission statement say? — "…reducing the extent of cancer as a health problem and the suffering it causes, through research, education and service." It seemed to Alison like that purpose was forgotten…and now the event was just about who could throw the biggest party!

Alison didn't know and didn't understand the significance of small town politics. She had supposed it was like running a small company, but she was finding that personalities played a bigger part in it than she thought. As she looked around at those gathered at here, she had no doubt that these clever and wily women would first do what was best for their own town…then, of course—as good neighbors do—help the next town over.

Finally, browsing to the end of the guidebook, Alison gave it back to Sally.

"These are expensive…are they reused for next year's event?" Alison said questioningly.

"No, I don't think so," Sally said. "Like I said, this is my fourth year as a committee chair, and I've never had to reuse a guidebook. Each year we get new ones with only slight changes to them…mostly there's a new picture on the cover. We get them free from our local community organizer who works for the NCA."

Alison's mind drifted. "But someone has to pay for them?" she thought.

"You'll meet him if you become a volunteer," Sally continued. "Who?" Alison asked.

"Mitch Cutter—he's our local community organizer. He drives over to Rosemont from the Front Range and checks on our progress once a month," Sally whispered.

Alison thought to herself, "Unbelievable!" She hoped the look on her face didn't give away what she was thinking. "How can that woman use the word 'local' when the NCA worker comes to Rosemont from the Front Range…yet *I* get called the outsider? That's nonsense!" But then she replied to Sally, with only mock surprise, "Really?"

"Oh, yes. This year, he told us we had to raise $35,000 or he wouldn't make his bonus."

Alison was incredulous. "What!?" she said a bit too loud. The conversation around the table stopped. Everyone looked at Sally.

"Oh, I'm sure he was just kidding about the bonus," Sally said apologetically to the others.

Alison had heard about the National Cancer Association from her many years at Merck Pharmaceuticals and some collaborative work she had done through the Jefferson's Kimmel Cancer Center in Philadelphia. She remembered there were mixed feelings about the organization from some of the researchers. She recalled it had something to do with the way it awarded grants. She made a mental note to call Rick, her old friend back at Merck who worked in the company's legal department, when she got home; he'd help jog her memory. She couldn't remember why she had never attended one of the many NCA fundraising events back in New Jersey; probably because she felt she had done her giving towards a cure for cancer with the many overtime hours in the lab, especially at Cyclacel, whose focus was in the area of the tumor-suppressing genes.

"Alison, are you ready?" Connie's question brought her attention back to the discussion.

"I'm sorry...ready for what?"

"Ready to sign on to one of the committees," Connie replied.

Alison, trying to buy more time—she wasn't really interested in any of the committees—hesitated for a moment, then said, "Well, I'm not quite sure...they all seem so interesting. May I just work with you, Connie? You said you could use the help," Alison responded. "That was a commitment without really commiting to anything," Alison thought.

"Sure," Connie said, "you're right...I *could* use the help."

Alison said, "Good-bye—nice meeting you," to each of the women as they filed out the front door of Connie's house. The meeting had lasted well over two hours. "Not the most efficient agenda," she thought. It seemed to Alison that most of the women were there to socialize and exchange rumors, and a few came out of curiosity, just to see what I was like. "Thanks, Connie, for an interesting afternoon. Let me know when you need help stuffing envelopes," she added jokingly.

"Tomorrow?" Connie asked in a pleading tone. "I'm scheduled at the regional NCA office to pick up supplies for the recruitment party scheduled for next week."

"Now what do I do?" Alison questioned herself. Dinah—yes! There is Dinah. "Well, how long will we be gone? Dinah can only stay alone, max, five hours, until I get a doggie door installed," she said to Connie.

"I think that's enough time," Connie smiled with relief.

That evening, Alison took Dinah on a long walk down Hartford Avenue to the bike path that ran along the river. It was a wonderful spring evening. The new grass was just pushing through the brown earth and there were new buds just forming at the tips of the lilac bushes that spotted each side of the bike path. Alison did her best thinking while on walks with Dinah.

"Thirty-five thousand dollars from a community that doesn't even have a recreational center for children. That *is* an ambitious goal. How is this small community expected to do that?" Alison thought. "Why would a national nonprofit organization go against a community's wishes and ask for the same event in a neighboring town? Who would profit from that? It seems counter to the mission statement of any volunteer organization. Connie seems intelligent and practical—why is she going along with this impossible goal?" Tomorrow, Alison knew she would have her opportunity to ask some questions on their drive to Fremont.

They continued walking as Alison thought. "Who else besides Rick did she know to call for information on the NCA?" Then it came came to her.

"Bill at Cyclacel, Yes—of course! How silly of me to forget Bill," Alison said aloud to Dinah, "Bill will know."

✑ Chapter Eight ✑

"Hi, Bill—it's Alison," she said enthusiastically. "Yes, I miss everyone, too. Dinah's fine and loves her big backyard. How's it going? Any breakthrough on the P54 clone? Oh, I'm sorry to hear that, but more sorry I won't be there when it happens…I know it will, hang in there."

The conversation continued a few more minutes, then Alison said, "Listen, Bill. I need you to look up some information for me. Remember how upset Jerry was last year?" Jerry was the newest post-doctorate scientist hired by Cylacel. He was young, brilliant and full of idealism. Alison was on the interview committee that reviewed his work and was very impressed with his thesis protocol.

"I recall it was about some grant he applied for from the National Cancer Association. Would you find out what that was all about? Oh, nothing. My new neighbor is involved in a fundraising event for them, and I just wanted to let her know what the money was being raised for…no hurry. Call me or email me when you find out something. Yeah…thanks. You'll have to bring the family out for a visit this summer, the kids would love the river. Remember the invitation is out there… You, too…'Bye now." Then Alison closed her cell phone.

Next, Alison called Rick at Merck laboratories. Rick was working late, as he always did on Wednesday nights. Alison felt lucky he decided to pick up the phone.

"Rick? It's Alison." Like Jack, Rick was a corporate attoney. His expertise was in the area of drug licensing. He had been on her advisory team for ten years when there was an issue of product labeling or naming. Because all inserts and patient instructions had to be signed off on by the legal department prior to submission to the FDA for approval, the legal departments worked closely with the scientists. For years Rick's keen legal mind had guided many of Merck's new drugs through the maze of federal requirements and FDA regulations. He also knew how dedicated Alison had been to her work and had been very disappointed when he heard she was leaving. She had kept in touch with him, even after she left Merck. There was an unspoken respect between the two of them that Alison always cherished. She missed that now. Once the catching up was complete, Alison said, "Rick, can you do me a big favor?"

"Of course," Rick replied.

"Find out what connections there are between the National Cancer Association and the National Institute of Health, the FDA, or the National Cancer Institute. No…nothing in particular, just general funding money…what kind of 'advocacy' they practice…ya know that kind of stuff…" Knowing Rick as well as Alison did, she knew he would want to know what initiated the interest, so she launched into telling him about Connie, the committee, and the NCA.

"Yes Rick, I'm trying to keep my questions to a minimum—they're really nice, intelligent people, so I can't figure out why they can't see it."

"Sure, Alison," Rick said. "I'll get back to you in a couple of days. We're in the middle of an orphan drug submission, and the deadline is in two days."

"I understand," Alison said. "Whatever you can find out… Thanks, Rick…you take care."

"You too," Rick said. Then Alison snapped her cell phone shut. Sitting there in her living room with one hand petting Dinah, she wondered what he would find.

ॐ Chapter Nine ॐ

*D*own *the rabbit hole…*

The next morning, Alison rose early. Knowing she would be gone most of the day, she wanted to go on a long walk with Dinah before leaving for Fremont. At 9 o'clock, Connie drove up the narrow driveway that connected to the path leading to the front porch. Dinah started barking before the doorbell rang. Alison hollered through the door, "I'll be right out!" Putting the Dobie in her crate, and handing Dinah a dog cookie, Alison spoke to her friend. "I'll be back early, Dinah, so have a good nap." She grabbed her purse and jacket and was out the front door.

"Have you ever been to Fremont?" Connie asked.

"Yes, I think so," Alison said. "Well, at least I drove through it on my way to Rosemont. I wanted to see Glenwood Canyon, so I came through Denver instead of going south."

"Yes, that is a pretty drive," Connie agreed. "Uh, I wanted to take this opportunity to apologize for Marge yesterday—that's just Marge," Connie went on. "I have known her all my life, and even though we don't belong to the same church, she's a good person. But, it's true! She has to be in the middle of every town activity. I suppose that's her insecurity. You'll see her leading the parade on Founders Day, too."

Alison politely laughed, thinking Connie was exaggerating to make her point. "No, I'm serious!" Connie snapped emphatically. "She *does* lead the parade. The town's folk know that's just the way Marge is and don't let it bother them. Her husband died two years before my John, and she was a great comfort to me."

"Oh, I'm sorry," Alison said sincerely. "How did John die?"

"Prostate cancer, same as Marge's husband," Connie said. "They were late in detecting it in Frank too," Connie added bitterly. For a while, there was silence in Connie's SUV.

"Connie, forgive me if I'm being nosy, but is that why do you do this?"

"Do what?" Connie asked…then realizing the question, said, "Oh, you mean *this*? Take on this year's fundraiser again?"

"Yes," Alison replied.

"Well, it started innocently enough four years back. John had died the year before and I had just retired from teaching. Nancy, one of the nurses at the Cancer Center who had been so kind to John, asked me to join her for lunch because there was someone she wanted me to meet. Well, I had known Nancy long before John was ever admitted to the Regional Cancer Center, so I agreed.

"We were joined by an employee of the National Cancer Association; I think her title was Regional Executive Director, or something just as pretentious." Connie gave Alison a glance as if to say she was not impressed.

"Anyway, I didn't know it before I walked in, but she was there to ask me to be the event chair for the National Cancer Association's first fundraiser in Rosemont. I remember she didn't ask right away; instead, we talked a long time about John. She asked more and more about his diagnosis and treatment, until both Nancy and I had tears in our eyes. Then she told us that more men will die of cancer unless we find a cure, and that the National Cancer Association is looking for a cure to cancer. That's when she asked if I would help.

"What was I supposed to say, Alison? Tell them that I didn't care about a cure for cancer?" Connie looked over at her for consensus. "Well anyway, that's how I got sucked in. Now everyone in Rosemont expects me to run it," she continued. "You know, that first year, NCA had me and all the committee chairs sign this commitment agreement. We all felt that if we said we would do it, then we had to sign, because here in Rosemont, your word is good—it means something. Well, I gave my word—not just to the NCA, but to the people of Rosemont." Connie again looked at Alison and, anticipating her remarks, said, "Oh, I know it's not a legal piece of paper, but to those of us who signed, it was even more important: It was more about our promise to the Rosemont community than the NCA.

"Right now, I still need a chairperson for the ribbon-running ceremony, and no one in that Fremont office will be happy when they learn we still need a ribbon-running chairperson."

"What's a ribbon-running ceremony?" Alison asked.

"Oh, don't worry about it—you'll learn soon enough. You'll also learn that those staff employees at the NCA do enough worrying for a herd of prairie dogs during a stampede." Alison laughed as she tried to picture the scene.

"Do the other women who chair committees feel the same as you?" Alison asked. "I don't really know," Connie replied. "I'm afraid if I show any doubt or reluctance, they'll all quit. Of course, rumors will spread that I am heartless and don't care about John's memory anymore," Connie went on. "You must have felt some guilt after you lost your husband," Connie said.

"Oh yes, sure I did," Alison replied.

"Well, then you know…," Connie said as she turned into the parking lot in front of a two-story brick building. "Here we are!" she said.

Deception in a Small Town

Connie gathered her papers and a binder from the back seat of the SUV and said, "Do you mind if I hurry ahead? The office is on the second floor."

"Oh sure, I have to make a phone call anyway," Alison said with a smile. She really didn't have to make a phone call, but she didn't want to be pulled into the meeting Connie was attending. She also wanted to see how available information was to someone who just happened to walk into a National Cancer Association office.

Alison waited about ten minutes, then went into the building and walked the stairs to the second floor. The office was well marked and the door was open. She walked in. The waiting area was very small, with two chairs and a small table in-between pushed up against the wall. No one was at the reception desk, but there seemed to be unfinished work lying on it, along with an open soft drink can and a couple of empty Snickers candy wrappers scattered on top of the open files. The opposite wall was covered with plastic slots; there were ten columns of slots running across the wall and five rows running down, each slot had a different brochure in it. It looked like a collection of colorful travel brochures.

Alison walked over and started browsing. One brochure was information on preventing skin cancer, another on diagnosing prostate cancer, and one even had instructions on breast self-examinations. There were brochures in Spanish, too. There was a section on "Services" that caught Alison's eye. Connie had mentioned the lack of NCA services in rural communities, so Alison was very interested in what kind of services might be available—especially for a rural community that had to raise $35,000.

"Whoooo are *you*?"

Alison whirled around to find a very large woman now sitting behind the reception desk "Pardon me?" Alison said.

"Who are you?" The words oozed from the mouth of the overweight middle-aged woman. Her greasy hair was gray turning into dirty blonde ends, as if someone had painted it then forgot to finish. She had it pulled back into a thin stringy ponytail wrapped with an elastic band

Alison studied the woman for a moment. It seemed that she had no neck, her head sitting right atop her very large body. She was obese. "The poor woman," Alison thought. "It must be a metabolic disorder." Alison began to consider the possible diseases she could be suffering from. She could only see her from the waist up; the desk hid her true size. She hoped she wouldn't get up from behind the desk. "I can see quite enough from here," Alison said to herself. The woman wore a faded blue cotton t-shirt with a scooped neckline, which allowed the top of her huge bosom to be exposed in a mass of loose cleavage. The t-shirt seemed two sizes too small and clung to the folds of cellulose that encircled the woman's middle. Alison became distracted by it—were there four or three folds? She couldn't tell. Then the woman asked again, "Who are *you*?"

"Can this woman really be the receptionist?" Alison thought. "Excuse me," she said to the woman. "I'm confused: Do you work here?"

"What do you mean by that? Explain yourself," was her defensive reply.

"Well, I'm just here to find out what services the National Cancer Association has to offer our community," Alison responded.

"Who are yoooooouuu!?" the woman said again, glaring at Alison.

"How can this rude, obnoxious, ill-mannered person be of any help to anyone?" Alison thought to herself. This woman was trying her patience. She felt like walking out of the waiting room and waiting for Connie by the car. But then that wasn't fair to Connie, and besides, if she did, this slug of a woman would prevail. So Alison decided against leaving and said curtly, "My name is Alison. May I wait for Connie here?" The woman's eyes disappeared into her face as the sides of her mouth turned up into a smile.

"Of course you are, and we are the National Cancer Association."

As Alison waited, she started reading the brochures. She must remember to ask Connie how available they were to the public. She certainly didn't want any more conversations with the "blue slug," the nickname Alison now gave to the metabolically challenged woman behind the desk.

All of a sudden, there was some commotion coming from one of the back offices. "I can't wait...I can't wait!" Alison heard the shouts. Then the words, "...The paper isn't straight...it's not straight and it must be straight-straight-straight!" again shouted out by the same loud, frustrated voice. The source of this noise soon became clear, for at that moment, from around the corner, came a short plump woman with short white hair, ranting and throwing her hands in the air then down to her side, then up went her hands again. She repeatedly shouted the phrases, "I can't wait! ...It's not straight!" The woman rushed through the waiting room past Alison and went down another hallway—not even noticing Alison sitting there.

The blue slug looked up from her work and said, "The copy machine is in the next room," pointing in the direction the short woman had rushed from, as if that explained the ranting woman's rude behavior. Alison nodded to the blue slug but remained silent. "How bizarre," Alison thought to herself. Connie was right about the people in this office.

Connie came out about a half-hour later; the look on her face was one of exhaustion. Not wanting to pile on with more questions, Alison simply waited for her instructions. Connie had her load a stack of boxes into the SUV. They were all labeled "Made in China," "Fulfillment Items," and "National Cancer Association." Again, Alison found the whole thing strange and inconsistent. "Why would an American-based organization not support American-made products, especially when the support comes from donated dollars?" Alison thought.

"Well, that's everything," Connie said with a forced smile.

Alison felt it might not be a good time for a heavy discussion, so she simply said, "They certainly have a lot of cancer information for the public. I was most interested in reading about the services they offer. I took a few brochures with me."

Connie looked over at Alison, saying, "Well, we used to get the brochures free, when we requested them. We would take them to the county health facilities, school district infirmaries, and hospital waiting rooms. The nurses and administrators in some of the rural towns really appreciated the patient information, because it was supporting their efforts with health education, especially with skin cancer.

"But the brochures aren't free anymore. When the National Cancer Association started charging the county and hospital for them, we stopped getting them. The county and schools now get their information free from other sources like the National Cancer Institute—they offer some wonderful patient information, just like those brochures from the National Cancer Association. Who knows why the resources are duplicated?"

"Not a good marketing decision," Alison thought to herself, recalling the organization's mission statement. But then, nothing seemed to make much sense.

"What about these services?" Alison asked. "Like road to recovery, and support for survivors?"

"Oh, Rosemont already has many of those services…it's called 'helping your neighbor,'" Connie said sarcastically. Then, after a brief pause, "I'm sorry," she said apologetically, "I didn't mean to be rude. You have no idea how a small community works, or what its needs are—and neither does the National Cancer Association."

Connie had something on her mind and Alison sensed she should just listen.

"I was dreading that meeting today for good reason," Connie said. "I knew that Mitch Cutter was going to be there."

"Is he the local community organizer Sally told me about?" Alison asked.

"Yes, but I didn't know the Income Development Director was going to be at the meeting."

"Income Development Director? My, my—that's quite a title. Certainly seems like they come up with some good ones, don't they?" Alison said.

"Oh, you wouldn't believe the titles some of them have. Do you know what a Distinguished Events Director does?" Connie rhetorically asked. "How about a Patient Embassador or Quality of Life Advisor? Then there're all the different levels of directors. Of course, you have the District Executive Director, then all the others—directors for this and directors of that. In addition, there are Vice Presidents for each Region, and the lists go on and on. Most of those at middle level management don't stay very long with the organization, only a year or two—I don't know why, but that's just been my experience. But I've heard the same from other volunteers across the state. In just this area alone, we've had two area directors in just four years...and that's when I stopped paying attention to who's who in the NCA," Connie said, now on a roll.

"What steams me," she continued, "is that they have no idea what a rural community needs in the way of cancer prevention or screening. I remember, after our first fundraising event three years ago—we raised $21,000—some of the staff at the hospital sat down and told representatives from the National Cancer Association what the area needed and wondered if they would help. The Cancer Center was asking for another infusion chair for the outpatient clinic and a mobile mammography machine. The mobile mammography machine could travel around three of the counties. Here in rural Colorado, getting to those women in the outlying areas can be the challenge, ya know?"

"Of course," Alison said in agreement.

"Well, I have never seen such condescension and arrogance on anyone's face as on the faces of those people from the NCA! Do you know what they told us after we had raised all that money?" Connie asked rhetorically. "They told us that they could not help us, because it wasn't the direction the organization wanted to go—but if our community ever got the mobile mammography machine, they would be glad to endorse it by putting their logo on the side of the van. Can you imagine?"

"Seems that their only interest is in giving the public the impression that they are helping the community...but their real interest seems to be in the money they can squeeze out of everyone," Alison said.

"Exactly!" Connie said. What Connie had just told Alison supported this, too. A working hypothesis was forming in her mind, but she would need facts to prove it.

"What are you going to do about it?" Alison asked.

"Not much I can do. I can't quit, because folks will ask why...and I've already explained how the rumors would start," Connie said.

"What about the hospital staff? What did *they* think about the lack of help from the NCA?"

"That's beyond me...I can't figure that part out. Maybe they just wanted to keep their jobs. No one will say anything, so that's how the rumors get started," Connie said. "Must be something political, or the hospital administrators are afraid of the National Cancer Association. They are a pretty big bureaucratic organization with connections all the way to Washington, D.C., probably with a large Federal grant."

"Oh, really?" Alison replied, trying to sound surprised. She knew very well there was some sort of connection between this nonprofit organization and the Federal government. She was looking forward to hearing from Rick at Merck's legal department.

"Then again," Connie continued, as if talking to herself, "since we got the Regional Cancer Center, which was a joint venture between our hospital and the St. Johns Hospital in Fremont, ya know," she said, pausing to get acknowledgment from Alison, "the National Cancer Association has been trying to have more of a presence here in Rosemont ever since."

"So tell me about this Income Development Director," Alison asked, trying to change the subject.

"Oh, I'd rather not; it's such a waste of a nice drive home. Besides, you'll see her at the Recruitment Rally next week. You *are* coming?" Connie asked.

"You bet, I wouldn't miss it for anything," Alison said. "This is going to be interesting," Alison thought to herself.

The rest of the way back to Rosemont, Connie and Alison chatted about gardening and what vegetables grew best at this altitude. They talked about the upcoming events in town, such as the car show and the quilt show, and the farmers market that was held every Saturday morning starting in June. Alison was looking forward to it all and decided that Connie, while lacking some diplomacy, had a good heart and was a good person—one that she hoped she could call a friend.

ca Chapter Ten so

That evening Alison got on the internet and checked her email—nothing yet from Rick or Bill—then she started googling nonprofit organization." She landed on a great website, www.coloradononprofits.org, and was surprised at the statistics for the last year, 2005. Nonprofit organizations in the state of Colorado accounted for a $13 billion industry and employed thousands of people. Alison had no idea that they made up such a significant economic entity in the state. She read on and learned that Colorado nonprofits attracted and brought in from out-of-state over $900 million. Alison reasoned that, with so many medical schools, hospitals, and research institutions in larger cities like Denver and Boulder, most of those dollars must be in the form of Federal funding for scientific grants and studies—not just in medical research. "If this is the third-largest industry in Colorado, imagine what kind of dollars were controlled by nonprofits in larger states like New Jersey," she thought.

As she browsed the website, she found hundreds of nonprofit classifications in the state of Colorado. The sectors she was most interested in were those that overlapped with the services the National Cancer Association claimed to offer. Alison found over 600 registered nonprofits in the county of Rosemont alone. Narrowing it down, she came up with five nonprofits that helped cancer patients through education, family support, financial aid, transportation, and home health care. These were the services that, according to Connie, the National Cancer Association promised to bring to Rosemont with their donated dollars—services that the folks in Rosemont had yet to see. The one goal included in the National Cancer Association's mission statement that seemed to be missing in Rosemont was cancer research, or even a drug trial. Alison looked down at the computer's digital clock and read 11:13. "Well, this'll just have to wait until tomorrow," she said to herself. She turned off the computer, let Dinah out one more time, then went upstairs.

❧ Chapter Eleven ☙

The next day, after her morning walk with Dinah, Alison put the Dobie in her crate. She had to remember to arrange to get the doggie door installed. With all the meetings and short trips with Connie, the summer would be half gone before she ever got it done. That morning, she tried to avoid the backyard—not wanting to be roped into an errand for Connie—which was out of character for Alison. She liked her neighbor as a friend, and in a way, she felt sorry for Connie's dilemma.

There were stops at the post office and the library; Alison wanted her library card. Rosemont had a very nice facility and a good collection of books and tapes. She had happened on their website while browsing the Internet the night before. Then she needed to go to the feed and grain store for Dinah's food; next, the hardware store for picture hooks—she just had to get her glass-framed photographs hung and off the floor

Alison enjoyed the morning, just driving through the streets of Rosemont. At one of the stop signs, she noticed the sign pointing to the local hospital. It was the same in every American town: a big white capital "H" set on a blue background. She turned down the street, and while she wasn't dressed for a professional visit, she decided to check it out. The next block over she saw the Regional Cancer Center. Alison decided to make it a short fact-finding inquiry. She parked her Jeep in the lot and went in.

There were a few elderly women in the small waiting room off to the right and a receptionist who greeted Alison with a pleasant smile, saying, "May I help you?"

"Well yes, I hope so," Alison said. "I just moved to Rosemont; I'm a widow and I'm wondering if I ever got cancer, who would be there to take care me…I have no family here." The receptionist, who was well groomed and very pleasant, took Alison's blunt remarks in her stride and replied, "Are you planning on getting cancer, Ma'am?"

"Oh, no—of course not," Alison blushed. "I was just wondering what services would be available to me if did…I have insurance, but who would take care of my dog? She's all I have."

"I see," said the receptionist. "Let me have you talk with our Resource Coordinator."

"Thank you," Alison said with a smile and went into the waiting room to sit down. She noticed plastic slots on the wall with pamphlets and brochures in them and went over to look through the literature. Selecting one, she sat down to wait, nervously fingering the brochure. She noticed it was actually a nicely done tri-fold in two colors—opening it, she started reading about a program called "Bosom Buddies." The brochure explained that they were a group of volunteers who offered a weekly support meeting to women dealing with breast cancer. "Wow," Alison thought to herself. "This is what Connie meant about neighbors helping neighbors." She read on—about the financial assistance they offer for mammogram screening and counseling services for family members; and hats and scarves for women going through the side effects of chemotherapy, and the fact that they helped over 70 women a year. "I had no idea breast cancer was so prevalent in such a small community," Alison thought to herself. Knowing this made it all very personal to her. She was very familiar with the pharmaceutical compounds, mechanism of action, and pharmacodynamics—of many of the drugs used to treat cancers. In fact, Alison remembered that last year at Merck, she was on the product team that brought Zolinza to market in the United States. She remembered it was approved for the treatment of cutaneous T-cell lymphoma.

But the needs of a patient fighting cancer go beyond the drug studies and treatment regimens. It's also about how cancer affects their families, the financial burden, and especially their dignity. Alison put the brochure down. "I had no idea…" she thought to herself. At that moment, a woman came into the waiting room and called out, "Alison?"

"Yes, that's me."

"My name is Clare. I'm the Resource Coordinator here. Judy, our receptionist, tells me you have some questions…would you like to join me in my office?"

"Yes. Thank you," Alison said, getting up, then followed the woman down the hall. Clare offered her a chair in front of a large desk, which had files neatly stacked on either side, and went behind it to sit down. Alison thought Clare to be in her late fifties, with short permed hair that must have been strawberry blonde a long time ago. Her eyes peered out over a pair of reading glasses, and their color matched the pale-green blouse she wore.

"So, what can we do for you?" Clare asked

"Well, first, let me say, I don't have cancer, but if I ever did get cancer, I wouldn't know what to do. You see, I am a widow who just moved here and have no family. I just read the brochure on Bosom Buddies, and I was very impressed by the way the people help their neighbors here in Rosemont."

"Why, thank you," Clare said with a modest smile. "We are pretty proud of the people in our small town. So Alison, where did you move from?"

"Rockaway, New Jersey," Alison replied, "and I have to say that in a larger community like Rockaway, if a person was diagnosed with cancer, there are public agencies to help them with services. These kinds of situations would be considered private matters, and not necessarily shared with neighbors."

"Well, in this town, Alison, people find out things, either at work or the grocery store, and most people want to help. Perhaps because that's the example they were shown as children, or perhaps it's the good feeling you're left with, knowing you have helped someone you know. It's a personal gift, not to be judged or analyzed," Clare said.

"Yes, I suppose you're right," Alison said, a bit embarrassed. "But who pays for it? The mammograms, and rental space for offices, and the support meeting…even those brochures aren't free."

"You're correct," Clare said, "Bosom Buddies is an all-volunteer organization with no paid personnel. It was started three years ago by a group of breast cancer survivors—myself among them—who realized the need for services here in Rosemont—the same services I needed when I was going through cancer treatment. The hospital could only do so much, and the Regional Cancer Center had just opened their doors, was still in need of staff and equipment. So, my friends and I then asked a number of larger organizations for financial help and a special bed for the clinic. Most of those national organizations are based in large cities; they didn't understand the needs of a rural community, and they refused to support us with those things. They turned a blind eye, so to speak.

"But that didn't make the needs disappear," Clare continued. "So we started our own 501-C3 with funds and volunteers from the surrounding area. The hospital gave us space for support groups and the Cancer Center did some printing for us. The volunteers joined mostly by word of mouth. We still receive no funds from governmental agencies. All of our money continues to be raised from the local general public, and it's only spent for the benefit of those in rural-area Colorado—especially women," Clare said, showing a hint of well-earned satisfaction.

"So, this is one of those 600 nonprofits in Rosemont County," Alison thought to herself. She was truly impressed at the tenacity and self-reliance this community had.

"Perhaps you will join us for our yearly fundraiser?" Clare asked.

Alison hesitated. "Of course, as long as there isn't any conflict with my schedule."

"Of course," Clare said.

Alison stood and held out her hand to Clare. "It was so nice meeting you. Everyone here is so nice—I'm sure there's something I can do."

"That would be wonderful," Clare said. "Thank you for taking the time to come in." Alison left and walked down the hall, thanking Judy as she passed the reception desk. Once outside in the parking lot, Alison looked at her watch and realized a whole hour had passed, and she still needed to go grocery shopping before going home to let Dinah out. As she drove, she thought about what she just learned. "What an amazing contrast between the National Cancer Association office in Fremont and the office I just left," Alison thought. How the folks in Rosemont step up to the plate, solving problems—something many of her former coworkers could benefit from. Which reminded her: She should have heard from Bill at Cyclacel by now.

That evening, Alison got back online and searched for sites listing the National Cancer Association. Immediately, the

Deception in a Small Town

Better Business Bureau website—www.bbb.org/us/charity—popped up. Curious, she typed in "National Cancer Association" on the query line, and a list of 66 affiliated locations popped up under that organization. Some were listed as national charities and others were listed as local charities. Searching for their financial reports, she narrowed her search and found only six accredited NCA affiliates with the BBB; not all of those listings had financial reports available. Alison wondered how the affiliates could be accredited without a financial report, since the BBB requires that certain financial standards be met before issuing accreditation. Continuing to read about the standards on the BBB website, Alison found two criteria. The first was that the charitable organization must spend at least 65% of its total expenses on program activities, and the second was that it must spend no more than 35% of related contributions on fundraising. "Related contributions" included donations, legacies, and other gifts received as a result of fundraising efforts.

"So, that means in order to stay in the good graces of the BBB, the local National Cancer Association can only spend 35% of what it brings in on the fundraising itself. That is very interesting," Alison thought to herself. "How does one find out how much is spent by an organization on a fundraiser if a financial report isn't on filed with the BBB?" Alison read on.

Other standards set out by the BBB that Alison found interesting had to do with financial reporting:

> *Make available to all, on request, complete annual financial statements prepared in accordance with generally accepted accounting principles.* When total annual gross income exceeds $250,000, these statements should be audited in accordance with generally accepted auditing standards. For charities whose annual gross income is less than $250,000, a review by a certified public accountant is sufficient to meet this standard. For charities whose annual gross income is less than $100,000, an internally produced, complete financial statement is sufficient to meet this standard.

"Maybe if this particular nonprofit creates more and more affiliates, and each one doesn't meet the requirement of $250,000 earnings, then that's how the organization sidesteps this requirement and can ignore the reporting standards," Alison reasoned. The following section contained more information:

Include in the financial statements a breakdown of expenses (e.g., programs, salaries, travel, etc.) that shows what portion of these expenses was allocated to program, fund raising, and administrative activities. If the charity has more than one major program category, the schedule should provide a breakdown for each category.

It all seemed like a shell game to Alison. But there was more:

*Include on any charity websites that solicit contributions, the same information that is **recommended** for annual reports, as well as the mailing address of the charity and electronic access to its most recent IRS Form 990.*

"Interesting choice of words— 'recommended' rather than 'required.' Some organizations probably take advantage of that wording," Alison said aloud. At least she knew Dinah was listening.

"I need a simpler approach," she thought. She continued to search other sites. A second independent website reported the NCA's funds for he fiscal year ending August 31, 2005. Alison read the listed allocations breakdown as being 70% of funds for Program Services; this was further divided into four categories: Research 14%, Prevention 20%, Patient Support 20%, and Detection and Treatment 16%. The remaining 30% was allocated to Supporting Services, and this was again further divided into Fundraising, 22%, and Management 8%.

"Well, that's good to know," Alison thought. It meant that the Better Business Bureau's Standards for Charity Accountability of at least 65% of expenses going into program services and no more than 35% to overhead and fundraising expenses had been met for 2005.

Deception in a Small Town

Alison considered what this meant. "So, in other words, if the community of Rosemont raised $25,000 last year, then as little as $3,500 might have gone to cancer research, while $5,500 went to fundraising," she thought. "That's ridiculous!" she said aloud, waking Dinah, who was sleeping on the floor next to the desk. She wondered if Connie ever did the math. "Fifty-six percent of $25,000 is $14,000. I wonder if the community of Rosemont saw any of that in the form of patient services, prevention, or treatment those funds were suppose to be spent on?" She wondered who that money could have helped at the Cancer Center. But that was something she would never know.

At the charitynavigator.org website, Alison signed on. There she entered in the National Cancer Association, and the organization's headquarters came up. There were three tabs at the top of this page, and she selected "rating." Up popped the financials for the headquarters of the organization. "Pretty impressive," Alison thought to herself. Then she returned to the previous page and clicked on "Comments." There were 42 listed comments, and Alison started reading them. They were from people who had cancer and detailed their experiences with the National Cancer Association. There was even a nurse who worked for the National Cancer Association who wrote in. Alison, having no personal experience herself with the organization, found the comments enlightening.

Then, under the organization's own website, Alison saw a news update that read, "Access to Care is the theme of the organization's new ad campaign. While not advocating a specific solution, the organization is looking to start a dialogue and increase the 'political will' needed to address the issue."

"How nebulous is that?" Alison thought to herself. But the words "political will" made her very uncomfortable and more suspicious. She would just tuck this information away for now and call Bill in the morning.

The next day, Alison got on the phone to Bill.

"Hey Bill—it's Alison. Ya got a minute?"

"Sure, I'm glad you called. You were on my list to follow up with today; you saved the company a nickel," Bill chuckled. "What I have is kinda vague, but I hope it helps. I talked to Jerry— our current boy-genius at the lab"—Bill added dryly, "And he told me that Thomas Jefferson University in Philadelphia has received an institutional research grant—what they call an "IRG"—from the National Cancer Association for $210,000 to be awarded over a three-year period. The director of Kimmel Cancer Center, Dr. Robert Peterson, who is a professor and chair of cancer biology at Jefferson Medical College, is the principal investigator on the grant. Dr. Marion Neilson is the co-principal investigator; she is an associate professor of cancer biology. Anyway, the award enables Jefferson to give small grants of $30,000 for salaries to each beginning investigator. As you know, Alison," Bill continued, "the definition of these beginning investigators is that they have no national peer-reviewed research grant support. The goal is to attract them into cancer research. Specifically, the IRG supports the development of newly independent investigators to conduct cancer research and fosters direct relationships between the research institution and the local NCA. This grant supports research by such investigators in areas of special interest to Jefferson *and* the National Cancer Association.

"Jerry was telling me this is great for any post-doctorate without an independent thought in his head, who isn't smart enough to apply for his own grant support, or who doesn't mind submitting to the antiquated theories that come out of the department of medicine. Jerry said the grants went for some research of special interest to the National Cancer Association, not for any leading-edge brilliant theorem such as the one Jerry presented.

"In a way, it was a blessing he was turned down, because Jerry would not have been allowed to follow his own protocols."

"What do you mean?" Alison asked.

"Jerry later learned that the grant recipients would be doing work based on a protocol written by one of the directors, and he would have just been a grunt technician in the director's laboratory with only a big title and his own office.

"That's why when we here at Cyclacel saw some of his work in protein separation and computer simulations of P54 structural arrangement, we grabbed him up. He's doing work in receptor proteins and mRNA that the university is still years from understanding.

"Jerry once told me he was so glad there were biotech companies with vision, and that he's doing some great things that the company hopes to bring to clinical trials in a couple of years."

"Yes, I know about the trials," Alison said as she paced back and forth in her living room. "I had no idea that the National Cancer Association could dictate the direction that cancer research takes."

"Well, I suppose it's their money…"

"Donated dollars!" Alison qualified.

"Still, they can do whatever they want with it…to a degree," Bill continued. "So, in other words, if they think that prostate cancer is more important than childhood leukemia, then they direct the funds to a favored institution, which then gets 10 to 15 % of the grant funds right off the top—as a line item expense for administrative purposes." Then Bill added, "It's SOP—standard operating procedure. You see, Alison, the more these institutions like the Thomas Jefferson University suck up to the NCA, the more grant money comes their way…it's just survival, Alison, and it's legal," Bill said sympathetically.

"But people aren't told this. It seems that sets politics over purpose," Alison said disappointedly, thinking of the people of Rosemont who were raising funds for the NCA.

"That's about it, and that's what made Jerry so upset," Bill said. "You know, Jerry is such an idealist, he thinks everyone is as motivated as he is about finding new ways to treat cancer. He doesn't realize that some people are just in it for the money."

"That's a sad statement," Alison said.

"I know," Bill replied, "I don't mean to sound so cynical. I'm sure that these organizations do some good somewhere. I just know that in Jerry's case, the National Cancer Association missed a good opportunity because of their misplaced priorities."

"Thanks, Bill," Alison said. Then, trying to end the call on a happier note, she continued, "Hey, that reminds me…I have a good joke for you to put up on the board in the lounge. I'll send it, okay?"

"I'll look for it on my email," Bill replied. "Hey, you take care—we miss you here…I'll tell everyone things are going well for ya."

"Thanks again, Bill, for your help… Take care," Alison said, then put down the cordless. Tomorrow evening was Connie's Recruitment Rally, and she wanted to sleep on what she had just learned.

❧ Chapter Twelve ❧

The next day, Connie came over bright and early. Alison was expecting her and the front door was open. Dinah recognized Connie through the screen door, and her bark changed from a protective tone to a friendly tone.

"Hi, Dinah," Connie said. "Where's the boss?"

"Right here!" Alison said with a smile as she came around the corner from the kitchen. "Want some coffee before we go?"

"Sure…we should have time," Connie said, as she nervously played with a key that was in her hand. "I just picked up the key to the community center, but we can't get in until 10 o'clock." She seemed preoccupied. This was a relief to Alison, who wanted to avoid sharing the conversation she had with Bill yesterday. Alison was still not sure if she should tell Connie what she had learned.

"What's wrong? You seem nervous," Alison asked, concerned that her friend wasn't feeling well.

"Oh, nothing really. I don't know why I feel so pressured by the NCA. I am, after all, only a volunteer, but they push and push and I don't know how to say no."

"Who's pressuring you?" Alison asked.

"Well, staff from the NCA. Oh, it's not just the local community organizer, Mitch Cutter…"—the term "local" was so annoying to Alison— "…but Marcia Harris—she's the Income Development Director from the headquarters—and she works for the Vice President of the entire Colorado Division."

"Oh dear, another big title," Alison said flippantly, trying to make light of it for Connie's sake.

Connie understood Alison's efforts and smiled, saying, "Yes, another big title—and thanks—but with both of them coming to the rally this evening…well…you'll see what I mean."

"Okay," Alison said. "Remember, I'm here to help; just let me know what I can do. We're both volunteers," Alison said reassuringly. Attempting a half smile, Connie said, "Thanks, that helps. Once we get everything set up, we can leave and lock up later. I want to change before the rally, and…I know, I know—Dinah will have to be let out," Connie said with a laugh.

Alison laughed along with her as she led Dinah into her crate, saying, "It's just for a few hours, dear Dinah. I'll be home soon."

They both got into Connie's SUV that was so full of boxes, ice chests, banners, and flags that neither of the women could see out the back window. Connie had also loaded a dolly, and this was the first thing to be unloaded when they arrived at the Community Hall on the other side of town.

"Just load up the dolly with stuff while I open the doors and turn on the lights," Connie said.

"You got it, Sarge," Alison chimed back with a smile. She noticed that many of the boxes she was unloading were those that Connie had picked up in Fremont at the local office of the NCA. She headed in the direction that Connie had gone and found a pair of double doors that opened into a large room. Alison entered the room and found a stage at one end and a kitchen area at the other end. There were folding chairs and tables leaning up against the walls on either side.

Alison hollered, "Where does this stuff go?" Her voice sounded hollow in the large empty space.

From somewhere in the large room came Connie's voice hollering back, "Just start bringing everything in…place it to one side. We have to set up the tables and chairs before we can unpack stuff."

On the third load from Connie's SUV, Alison spotted a small helium tank. Curious, she asked, "What's that for?"

"For the balloons, of course," Connie replied with an incredulous look that prompted Alison to say, "Of course. Sorry." These people are serious about their meeting, Alison thought to herself.

Once the SUV was unloaded, Alison locked the doors and went back into the hall. Connie was studying the layout as she handed her the car keys.

"Thanks. Ya know…the first year, we had the tables and chairs along here," Connie said, pointing to one end of the room, "but people got in the food line before they signed in. We had more people than scanning forms, and that kind of stuff drives Mitch crazy. So this year, your table…or, rather, the sign-in table…will have to be visited first, before the food line. A lot of people just come for the food, ya know, and this year, we at least have to get their information on a scanning form before they get in the food line. I think this arrangement will also give the perception of more attendees," Connie added.

"Uh, how many people do you expect?" Alison asked, hoping it wouldn't be considered a stupid question.

"Well, that's just it. The committee hasn't signed up as many people as last year, but I have to make it look like we have more attendees than will really come…for the sake of Marcia Harris. You know, the Income Development Director I was telling you about," Connie said questioningly. "She'll report back to the district VP immediately after the meeting."

"Oh...of course. That makes it all soooo clear," Alison said sarcastically under her breath. "So...if she is an Income Development Director, I wonder if she can count?" The thought of a director of a national organization unable to count attendees at a meeting sounded so absurd to Alison that she burst out laughing...but she didn't want to point that out to Connie, who was now off in a different direction, opening other boxes.

The two women continued unfolding and setting up the large long tables; then they placed the folding chairs on one side of the tables. Connie seemed to be in a trance, visualizing the table arrangements. Alison remained quiet and just followed her lead. Once the tables were arranged to Connie's satisfaction, the women pulled out aqua-colored plastic tablecloths, opened them, and spread them over each table. Alison recognized this bright aqua color from the NCA's national logo. The color was on all the event booklets and must be for the purpose of identifying the NCA from other nonprofit organizations. Booklets were pulled from another box and placed like dinner mats on the tables in front of each chair, along with a pencil, a black pen, and little prizes. The little prizes came out of boxes marked "Made in China."

Alison was almost afraid to ask, but since she was unable to resist, she said, "What are those for?"

"Oh, those are gifts for the attendees," Connie replied. "Marcia and Mitch insist that everyone who comes get a prize or gift."

"Who pays for them...Mitch and Marcia?" Alison asked.

Connie stopped what she was doing. "There you go again," she said. "Aren't you going to ask 'why' as well?" she continued sarcastically. "Well, to answer your question, Alison, Mitch told us that these items are required expenses and they come out of the moneys we raise."

"Required?" Alison echoed. "Required by whom?"

"Required by the National Cancer Association, so our fundraiser can be classified as an official NCA event."

"Does Mitch or Marcia show you the expenses your fundraising event is charged?"

"I'll have to ask Libby about it. She's been the chair of the finance committee for the past three years. I remember last year, she told me that when she asked to see the expenditures, she was told by Mitch that it was NCA business and that he wasn't allowed to show them to her. He told her that her job was to raise money and not to worry about expenses.

"You'll learn that with Mitch and Marcia, it's always about the money. I've tried to protect the community from their priorities, but each year it becomes harder and harder, because the community isn't seeing any services come back to Rosemont like the NCA had promised."

Alison said nothing. Connie continued, "I heard of other finance committee chairs from other communities being shown the expenses charged against their fundraiser, so I know it's been done…it may just be up to the individual NCA organizer." From what Alison had learned online last night, she knew that financial disclosures should be open to the public, available to the people who donated money. They had a right to know how it was being spent. Alison thought about showing Connie the BBB website but decided against it. What did she expect Connie to do about it? Alison now could sense the bullying and pressure that was being put on Connie by Mitch and Marcia, and she was getting a clearer picture of how the organization operated. Was this the "political will" she had read about on the NCA website? "It sure fits!" she thought. Then, remembering she was only a newcomer in Rosemont, Alison simply acknowledged Connie with, "Oh."

Prizes were placed in front of each chair and boxes of Kleenex tissue were placed on the tables—three per table—then glitter was sprinkled around the tissue boxes.

"What are those for?" Alison asked, afraid of what she would hear.

"Wait…you'll see," Connie said, not even looking up from her work. "Help me put up these banners, will you?"

They worked most of the afternoon. The final items to set up were the food table and the audiovisual equipment. While Alison worked on the food table, Connie disappeared to set up the projector and screen and hook up the CD player to the sound system in the hall. Alison set out the chafing dishes and two large ten-gallon refreshment canisters. Then came the plastic plates, forks, and spoons, and paper cups and napkins. All the plastic items were either white or an identifiable aqua blue.

Connie showed Alison how to use the helium tank and fill the white and aqua balloons. Alison focused on her job, all the time mulling over the volumes of irregular and inconsistent information she was mentally processing. This was nothing like any science conference she had ever attended. She wondered what the PhDs would think if party whistles and glitter appeared on the conference table at the protocol presentation. She had to save that thought and suggest it to Bill next time they talked. That brought a smile to her face.

The final task before leaving the hall was to check all the forms and brochures at the sign-in table. This was where Alison knew she would be helping that evening. She also knew that Connie would not have time later to explain the form and the filing system, so she insisted Connie show her before they left the hall. There was an accordion file and a box organized with tabs separating other files. But the form that most interested Alison was titled, "Participant and Survivor Registration," and next to the title was a bar code. There was a line to fill in "Name of Squad" and square boxes for individuals to print in their name, address, phone number, and email address. Then below that was a request for birth date, race, and the reason for attending the event with four choices offered. Then there was a section on medical information, with a space for "diagnosis"—Alison assumed this was for a cancer diagnosis—and the date of onset. The form asked for type of cancer and listed the six most common. There was also a box you could mark that was listed as "other." Alison wondered why this information was being requested. "It can't have anything to do with the event," she thought. "Maybe it's just a way to build a national data base for donation requests through the mail, or maybe they sell the information to insurance companies." At that thought, she felt a knot in the pit of her stomach. Alison knew that the Health Insurance Portability and Accountability Act—HIPAA, enacted by Congress in 1996—helped individuals and their families keep their medical information private. HIPAA established regulations for the use and disclosure of Protected Health Information, and Alison knew that that included an individual's medical record and payment history.

"But if an individual innocently gave the information to a third party such as the National Cancer Association, thinking they were just signing up for a charity event…hmmm… I wonder how this information is used by the National Cancer Association?" Alison said quietly to herself.

As a third party that received the information freely from individuals, could the National Cancer Association do whatever they wanted with it? Were charities covered by HIPAA regulations? Alison wasn't sure, but just the possibilities made her very uncomfortable.

"Alison…now this form must be filled out completely, by everyone, okay?" Connie was saying, picking up the form. "If they are part of a squad, have them write the name here," Connie said as she pointed to a section on the form. "If the forms aren't filled out completely, Mitch and Marcia will have a fit…not a pretty sight, I assure you."

"I can only ask them…I can't force them, can I?" Alison replied. "Just do your best," Connie said with a smile. After showing Alison how the files were organized, both women left the hall.

"We'll have to be back by 4:30 with the food and refreshments."

"Oh, what are you serving?" Alison asked.

"Pasta, salad, and bread sticks," Connie said as she scanned the room, mentally checking items off her list.

"...and what goes in the large canisters to drink?" Alison asked.

"...Kool-Aid," was the reply.

~ Chapter Thirteen ~

A Kool-Aid Party…

At 4:30, Connie drove up Alison's driveway. She honked the car horn and Alison came out. Wearing a slimming rayon floral dress and sandals, Alison felt she would blend into the crowd. After all, she hadn't worn a business suit or heels since she left New Jersey.

"Oh, you look nice," Connie told her.

"Thanks," Alison said with a smile, "and so do you, my dear." Connie was dressed in a two-piece casual skirt and top.

"Thanks," Connie replied, returning the smile. During the short trip to the Community Hall, there was little conversation, and Alison could tell Connie's mind was elsewhere. Arriving at the hall, there was a large white SUV in the parking lot. Connie pulled in next to it. Alison noticed it was a new Cadillac Escalade…their top of the line.

"Whose is that?" Alison asked.

"That must be Mitch's rental car."

"I wonder who pays for that?" Alison thought to herself.

Connie looked over at Alison and, seeing the look on her face, added, "I know…I thought the same thing. But we were told the staff of the NCA gets a corporate rate, so the management at the National Cancer Association allows the staff to rent anything they want when they travel. Mitch says the bigger cars are safer on the road."

Alison didn't want to think about that now. She was simply stunned. Without a word, the two women began carrying the pans of pasta and salad into the hall. Once inside, Alison saw a large man fiddling with a computer that was now plugged into the extension cord Connie had brought in earlier.

"Hi, Mitch!" Connie called out, the words echoing in the empty room.

"Hi, Connie," the man said without turning around, his words followed by trailing laughter that also echoed. "Just loading the new video I brought with me. It's from an event…last year's…somewhere in Ohio, I think. Wait'll ya see it…it's a real tearjerker! Oughtta get them really fired up to raise that money…right?" Mitch said. Again, a forced laugh followed his words like a laugh track in a TV comedy show.

"Mitch, this is Alison, a neighbor of mine. She's here to help," Connie said.

Mitch looked up from his fussing, seeming a bit annoyed by the interruption. "Oh, hi Alison…uh…nice to meet you."

From the graying around his temples, Mitch seemed to Alison to be in his mid-forties. He was neatly dresses, well-groomed and pleasantly overweight, "But that doesn't seem to slow him down," she thought as she watched him leave the projector and begin to bounce around the room, checking this and that. He fussed with each chair and rearranged some of the items on the tables. He tugged at the plastic tablecloths, removing the few remaining wrinkles. He reminded Alison of a nervous mother-of-the-bride before the wedding.

"Where is she? Where is she? Where is that Marcia Harris? She's late…she's late," Mitch said nervously as he again approached the two women, his eyes scanning the room. "People will start arriving soon. Oh, how I dislike doing things at the last minute…last minute…," Mitch repeated again and again, wringing his hands. This time the expected trailing laugher was slightly subdued. Alison was amazed by this odd behavior.

"We haven't seen her," was Connie's deflated reply. Alison could tell Connie's feelings were hurt. She had spent the entire day setting up for the NCA Recruitment Rally in the hall, knowing how Mitch was so focused on detail, and now he said nothing about it—no compliments, no polite acknowledgement, not even a kind word of appreciation. At that moment, Alison felt sorry for Connie. She probably took all of Mitch's fussing as criticism of her work. "I would too," she thought.

Around 5 o'clock, Mitch turned on the CD player that Connie had hooked to the sound system in the hall. Loud music started playing; it had a pounding fast-paced beat. Alison found the music irritating; it made it hard for her to hear the questions from the people now standing in front of her. Looking up from her check-in table, she saw Mitch near the microphone, clapping and bouncing to the beat of the music, the big National Cancer Association logo filling the screen behind him. He kept glancing at his watch. "He's probably still waiting for Marcia," Alison thought. Through the gathering crowd, she noticed a short red-headed woman quickly walking up to Mitch. She looked young—but then, at Alison's age, everyone looked younger. Alison thought the woman could be no more than 30 years old. She was petite and wore stretch hip-hugging slacks that were very trendy, along with a paisley three-button vest with the tails of a white dress shirt sticking out from under it. She had long gold chains wrapped around her neck that swung back and forth as she trotted out in a pair of open-back, two-inch heels. Her red hair was loosely tied on top of head like a pair of rabbit ears, and it appeared to Alison that it could use a good brushing. Last time she saw someone dressed like this, she'd been in a south Jersey mall.

Deception in a Small Town

"This must be Marcia," Alison thought. "Does she realize how utterly ridiculous she looks...how inappropriately she's dressed?" She looked around at the people with their paper plates, now sitting or mingling around the tables, hoping she wasn't the only person starring at this pretentious young woman. But most people seemed to politely ignore how she was dressed and what Alison considered her inconsiderate manner. She felt embarrassed for the woman, now standing with Mitch. Mitch looked angry—very angry—and was now throwing his hands around madly. But this time not to the beat of the music, which was still playing loudly. He and the woman seemed to be exchanging harsh words. Mitch shoved the face of his wristwatch at her and began tapping it during the exchange.

"How unprofessional of those two," Alison thought. "How simply rude and unprofessional." It appeared to her that they were behaving as if it was all about them. Another man then joined them, and Mitch stopped talking. The three of them walked over to the side of the room and continued a conversation. "I wonder who that is?" Alison said to herself.

After a moment, the music was turned down, and Mitch returned to the microphone. Most of the people had been through the food line and were now seated at the tables. Connie had managed to direct most everyone to the center tables in the room, so the tables in the back were the only ones with open seating. Mitch started tapping the microphone,

"Testing, testing...."

"Welcome, welcome, welcome, citizens of Rosemont, welcome to all," he said in a sing-song voice, with only a small giggle trailing his words. There was polite applause from the audience. "Now that everyone has their food and is seated, I would like to introduce a very special guest with us this evening. He will be sharing some very important information with you." The other man who had been standing with Mitch and Marcia joined Mitch at the microphone.

"This is Alan Gross, and he is your local volunteer liaison," Mitch said. "He's also a volunteer like you, but he works at a higher level—and on your behalf, of course. So, if you have a chance after the program, come by and say hi to Alan." Mitch turned to the man standing with him and started clapping quickly into the man's face, then he turned to the audience, encouraging them to join in. Once the polite applause had dwindled, Alan Gross took the microphone.

"Thank you all for coming this evening. I want you to know that I am also a volunteer with the National Cancer Association. My reason for being a volunteer is that I know what good work this organization does by supporting cancer research, and we all want to find a cure for cancer—don't we?"

Alison watched the people in the audience as some heads agreed, bobbing up and down. Then Alan Gross brought out a stack of files; Alison thought there must be hundreds of them, because the stack looked almost three feet high. It was divided into three sections by colored construction paper. The first section, starting at the bottom, was the largest and ended with a bright yellow sheet of paper about two-thirds of the way up. The next one was almost as large and ended with a blue sheet of paper. The very top section of the stack of files was the smallest and was only a few inches thick.

"I suppose you're wondering what this has to do with cancer research?" the man asked the audience. "Well, what you see here," and he pointed to the stack of files, "represents the many research projects that have been proposed. The stack represents the requests received by the National Cancer Association for funding last year alone. There are hundreds of thousands of scientists needing money do their work. The National Cancer Association would like to fund them all, but unfortunately there isn't enough money to fund all the scientists. So, all the projects aren't funded. This second group of files represents those projects that the National Cancer Association feels have merit. These are the ones we would like to fund, but again the money is not there. This last small stack on the very top represents those projects that have been funded by the National Cancer Association with the money you raised at the March at Night event." Alison was waiting for a rabbit to come out of the proverbial hat. "The National Cancer Association is asking your help. If you want to find a cure for cancer, then we need money to do it. What if the cure was in one of the files down here?" The man then pointed to the middle of the stack of files. "What if the cure to cancer lies in this project here?" The man pulled out a file from the middle of the stack, like a magician removing a tablecloth without disturbing the place setting that lay on top. "What if this project is the one, and we'll never know because we couldn't fund it because you didn't raise enough money?"

The man paused for effect; the silence was as if he was scolding them like children. "But, if you make your goal here in Rosemont, we may be able to fund this project," and he began to wave the file over his head. "Every dollar will get us closer to funding all the projects in the stack you see in front of you. Remember, the *one* cure for cancer may be funded with money you raise at this event. Now, who will join me in finding a cure for cancer?"

Alison was amused by this dog and pony show, knowing that that's not how it works. The man was given polite applause and Mitch was again at the microphone. "Thank you...thank you. I know Alan appreciates everything.

"Now we're going to show a short video of one of our more successful night marches—remember, success is what we strive for, right Rosemont?" Mitch asked.

"Right" was the weak response of a few seated in the room.

He repeated the question again, "Success is what we march for, right?" A few more responded from the audience. Mitch repeated the question again and again until everyone in the room loudly responded together, "Right!"

Then the lights dimmed and a change of music began. Alison had managed to get some salad and bread sticks before the lights went out and was now sitting in the back at a table by herself. There, filling the screen, was the National Cancer Association logo. The female narrator of the video began telling of the wonderful work done by the NCA and continued with stories of the many lives saved through their work. She must have repeated the name dozens of times as scenes of people walking or marching hand in hand around a dirt track or hugging on some athletic field flashed on the screen.

"So that's the big event," Alison thought to herself. Next, the narrator starting talking about all the cancer research supported by the NCA, and scenes of bald-headed children in hospital beds flashed up on the screen. Then the music slowed and became soft and calming. There was a chorus humming in the background as the narrator spoke of the lives saved by the NCA, and the scenes of these children again flashed on the screen. Alison had to admit that it was very emotional, and she was almost moved to tears. "So that's the reason for the Kleenex," she thought. Mitch was right, it really did tug on your heartstrings. The room was as quiet as a dormouse, and she could hear a few sniffles coming from one of the tables in front of her. Then the scene switched back to the March at Night event and the narrator asked for help from everyone...to support the good work of the National Cancer Association. The narrator continued to ask, "If you want to find a cure, then join the National Cancer Association on their march through the night and raise money to cure cancer."

The music rose to a crescendo and then ended. Alison thought it all seemed quit compelling. The lights in the hall were brought up. Mitch was at the microphone and immediately introduced Marcia Harris. There was polite applause from the group as she came to the microphone. Watching the crowd, it was obvious to Alison that this woman would never win the People's Choice award.

"Thank you…thank you," Marcia said in a real Texas drawl. "It is so nice to be with you again in little ol' Rosemont."

The music began again, this time a soft instrumental; Alison heard violins and piano.

"Now, we're all here tonight because y'all have been touched by cancer, so if your spouse is sufferin' or died from cancer, please stand up for me and the National Cancer Association. Come on…come on now…don't be shy. " Alison noticed a few people were standing now; Connie and Marge were among them. Marcia continued, "If you have lost a mother or father to cancer please stand." Then she said, "If you have lost a brother or sister…" She continued the litany until everyone in the room was standing, then she bowed her head for a moment. Looking up she said, "Now stay standing, please."

Then, stretching her arms out towards those standing like Moses parting the Red Sea, Marcia said, "Look around. Y'all are not alone. Y'all share the same hope, and that's to find a cure for cancer."

The people in the room all looked around at each other. Some of the women still with tissue in their hands were wiping their noses, and from the back where Alison watched, sniffles could still be heard. "Quite the little drama queen. She'd be better off in a theatre production," Alison thought to herself.

"Your fundraising dollars to the National Cancer Association will be turned into a cure for cancer. That's what we're gonna do. Right?"

Alison wanted so badly to stand up and ask Marcia Harris how she intended to do that. Or what percentage of money taken from this community actually went to research…or to rural community services, for that matter. Alison wanted statistics and facts. She looked around at these wonderful people in her new community and thought, "They're buying it…hook, line, and sinker, just like Connie did four years ago. Maybe they don't want to know the truth. Maybe it's all about the emotion and the feelings and remembering those who died from cancer. Maybe they don't want to admit how utterly helpless they feel…maybe this is their way of replacing that feeling of helplessness with one of doing something…anything that they've been told is good and useful."

Then Mitch joined Marcia at the microphone, and Alison's thoughts came back to the present.

"So how are we going to cure cancer?" Mitch asked the audience, and Marcia answered with, "Make our dollar goal!"

"Tell me again—How're we going to cure cancer?" Mitch's voice boomed over the loudspeakers.

"Make our dollar goal!" Marcia answered, gesturing to the group to chime in as Mitch kept repeating, "How are going to cure cancer?"

Those still standing chimed in along with Marcia, "Make our dollar goal!" The music changed to a fast upbeat tempo that continued as the group answered back to Mitch, who was now clapping with the music, "Make our dollar goal!"

This recruitment meeting with all the loud music and repetitive chanting, with arms waving, reminded Alison of the revival meeting scene in the movie *Apostle* she had seen with Jack in 1997. Alison couldn't figure out what all this had to do with statistics and the NCA's currently funded research. "What nonsense," she thought. She wanted to leave this ridiculous meeting but knew Connie's feelings would be hurt. So she stayed, wondering what absurd event she would witness next. She was relieved when Mitch and Marcia began to thank…"those of you who came tonight." The meeting was almost over. Alison looked at her watch; two hours had passed. She saw Connie coming over.

Deception in a Small Town

"Well, what did you think?" Connie asked.

Avoiding a truthful answer, Alison replied evasively, "Uh,...do you think I could chat with Mitch for a moment before he leaves?"

"I'm sure it would be okay. I'll ask him when we start the clean-up." Then, almost as an afterthought, Connie asked, "How many scan sheets did you collect?"

"Well, there are about ten squads...and 90 scan sheets," Alison replied.

Connie shook her head, saying, "They won't be happy...but then, they're never happy."

"I'll start gathering the paperwork on the sign-in table," Alison offered with an encouraging smile. Connie responded with the same half smile and walked back to the crowd of people still milling around. Alison stood at the end of her sign-in table, collecting the papers and thanking those who had come as they filed out of the Community Hall. She could hear car engines starting up and noticed some people still lingering in conversation near their cars. Within 15 minutes, the hall was empty of attendees. Sounds began to again echo as emptiness filled the room. Now that the people were gone, Alison waited, hoping she could chat with Mitch about the NCA's funding for cancer research. He was unplugging the computer and gathering the electrical cords from the CD player. He was humming a familiar childhood tune that Alison recognized; it was the tune to "Twinkle, Twinkle Little Star," but the words weren't familiar. She moved close enough to hear,

"Welcome, welcome silly people...
Food is serving, bellies full.

Sign right here, tell us all
Hmmm, hmmm, hmmm, hmmm.
Music playing makes them cry,
Shining dollars in the sky.

Welcome, welcome silly people.
Money comes—emotions high.

"What're you singing?" Alison asked in an attempt to engage Mitch in conversation.

"Oh, just a tune I learned while training for this job," he said, not looking up from his work.

"Mitch, I was wondering if I might ask a few questions about the research funded by the NCA," Alison said timidly. Mitch looked up,

"Questions, questions...so many questions—let's see...." He was counting on his fingers now. "There are nice questions, easy questions, hard questions, mean questions, questions with no answers, and questions with many answers. What kind of questions do you want to ask?" Mitch rhythmically replied, followed by a high-pitched laugh track.

"I hope a simple one," Alison answered cautiously. Mitch seemed to glare at her, almost daring her to speak. She continued, "Well, the way I figure it, based on data from your own website and the Better Business Bureau information on your organization, if this community raises $35,000—which is the goal they were given by the NCA, right?—then actually only $5,250, or 15%, will go to an institution or university for cancer research. But you led the people here to believe that *all* the money goes to cancer research. I'm confused—is it all or 15%?" Alison asked politely.

Assuming he was following her logic as she layed out her case, Alison continued, "...so, if only 15% is earmarked for cancer research, then where does the rest of it go? Are there measurable results that have come from the funds already raised from this community? And when will Rosemont see some of the services the NCA says they will provide? And...."

"Silly questions—silly, silly questions," Mitch interrupted in a dismissing arrogant manner. "I said nothing about funding cancer research—that was Alan Gross...and he doesn't work for our organization. He's only a volunteer and can tell you anything he wants. Don't you know *we* are the National Cancer Association? We raise money to cure cancer." Then, with a challenging glare, Mitch said, "You *do* want to cure cancer, don't you?"

"Of course," Alison replied, "but how does the NCA cure cancer with money? I thought it was the dedicated scientists in universities and pharmaceutical laboratories who find cures and treatments for cancer. The NCA doesn't cure cancer."

"Not true," Mitch countered sharply. "The National Cancer Association *is* the organization that gives the scientists their money so they *can* cure cancer."

"So, if the NCA gives the university scientist the money, does that mean that it can dictate to the scientists what kind of research to work on?" Alison asked rhetorically. "A simple question," she thought, not wanting to tip her hand and reveal all she knew on the subject—or her background.

Mitch was now looking annoyed and agitated, his eyes piercing, jaw set. This time there was no laugh track, only an ugly, very condescending tone in his voice. He was studying her now, wondering who she was. Then he said smugly, "You must be new to Rosemont—and obviously a very naïve woman. It's not about what is real...it's about perception—the perception of the people—and if the people think we cure cancer, then we take their money and let them think we cure cancer."

Mitch continued to glare at Alison, again with a look so sinister it made her shiver. He was daring her to respond. Then a wicked grin came over his face, and he added, "Don't even think about saying anything—no one will ever believe you...we *are* the National Cancer Association." Then he strutted off.

Alison was stunned. These people are frauds! She considered her options. She knew Mitch was right: No one in town would believe her if she repeated what she heard. She was a newcomer to Rosemont, and challenging these local people with the truth would not help her make friends.

For the next half-hour, Alison remained in a dazed state of mind while she and Connie broke down chairs and tables and returned them to each side of the hall. Mitch, Marcia, and Alan Gross all left well before cleanup was over. But Alison preferred to work with Connie and not with the staff of the NCA. "I'm sure glad that's over," Connie said as they loaded the back of her SUV. "Well, did you get your questions answered?"

"I sure did. Are all the NCA staff like Mitch?" Alison asked.

"I don't know…maybe we just got lucky!" Connie flippantly replied. Then the two women, as if reading each other's minds, looked at each other and started laughing.

∞ Chapter Fourteen ∞

Over the next few weeks, the weather warmed. It seemed like one morning there were leaves on the trees outside Alison's window, when they hadn't been there the day before. Today was Saturday, and she decided she must find someone to cut her lawn, which was now almost five inches high. After her morning coffee, she dressed, fed Dinah, and ate a quick breakfast of cereal and juice. She put the Dobie on her leash and went out. She walked down Hartford to the corner of Second Avenue, then around the corner to Third, when there in the yard she spotted him: His name was Jimmy, she soon found out, and he was mowing the lawn in front of a two-story white house on the corner. She stood there a while until Jimmy noticed her and turned off his power mower. "Good morning," Alison said.

"Mornin' to you, too," Jimmy said. Jimmy, 13 years old, had short blonde hair and wore a clean white t-shirt over a pair of cut-off baggy jeans.

"Looks like you're doing a great job," Alison said.

"Thanks," Jimmy said with pride. "I do my best…at least I try."

Alison enjoyed the honesty.

"What's the dog's name?" Jimmy asked. "Is he friendly?"

"*Her* name is Dinah," Alison said with a smile. "Yes, she's friendly to most. I'll bet she'll like you," she said, inviting Jimmy over to meet Dinah. Jimmy walked over and the dog started wagging her stubby tail. He seemed calm and held out his hand for Dinah to sniff.

"I think she likes you," Alison offered. "By the way, my name is Alison—we just moved into the house on Hartford Avenue. Do you know the one?" she asked.

"The one with the overgrown lawn?" Jimmy asked.

"Yes," Alison said with a chuckle. "That's why I'm here. I was hoping I could hire you to mow it for me."

"Sure! I could always use the money."

"What do you charge?"

"Ten dollars?" Jimmy said.

"Front and back…?" Alison replied.

"Yup!"

"…edge trimming the pathways and driveway?"

"Yup!"

"You got the job!" Alison said, and she held out her hand to close the deal. Jimmy was beaming and took Alison's hand, shaking it with enthusiasm. "Can you come over this afternoon?"

"You bet!" Jimmy was smiling.

"Thanks, well…I have to keep walking…ya know—the dog," Alison said, hesitating. She said good-bye to Jimmy who scratched Dinah on the neck, then they continued down the street. She heard other lawn mowers buzzing from backyards and could smell the new-cut grass. This really felt like home.

ॐ Chapter Fifteen ॐ

The following afternoon Alison was in the yard weeding. Hearing the phone ring in the house, she slowly got up from her gardening and rushed towards the house, kicking off her clogs onto the porch before going inside. Dinah danced with excitement alongside.

"Hello?"

"Well, hello to you!" came the voice back. Alison knew exactly who it was and a broad smile came over her face. It was Rick.

"Hi, Rick—how are you? … Busy, I'm sure—with the latest drug application and the merger and…"

"So, why did you ask?" was the curt reply.

"Oh, I'm sorry, Rick. I guess I still have that bad habit of answering questions that I just asked."

"As long as you recognize the affliction…that's the first step on your 12-step recovery program," Rick replied in a fatherly tone. They both laughed at the reference to Alcoholics Anonymous and Alison's bad habit of anticipating replies.

The conversation moved to the gossip at Merck, Alison's replacement, and the news on the latest merger. Then Rick said,

"Now, to get to why I called. I have some interesting facts regarding the National Cancer Institute, which you know is a department under the National Institute of Health, which is under the Food and Drug Administration. "Yes, yes—go on," Alison said with anticipation.

"Do you remember, back in 1988, California voters passed Proposition 99?"

"Yes, it barely squeaked by…but what does that have to do with…"

"A little patience my dear," Rick said calmingly. "Proposition 99 was simply a huge increase in the state's tobacco tax, and it was sold to the voters of California as a way to stop kids from smoking. Well, it did slow the sales of cigarettes slightly, but what it also did was generate more money for the state, and that caused a lot of infighting among different California state agencies over allocation of those new tax dollars."

"How so?" Alison asked as she jotted down a few notes.

"Well, usually there are defined allocations in a proposition when tax increases are proposed. That wasn't the case in Proposition 99; it didn't define how the funds would be spent, and that's what caused different agencies in the state to argue over the new tax dollars—each wanted the money for their own programs. Well, this infighting brought unwanted media attention to the state agencies, and the public wanted to know how their tax dollars would be spent."

"I can see the messy PR that must have caused," Alison replied.

"Especially since some of those tax dollars raised went to organizations and programs that had nothing to do with public health."

"Kinda a payback for their support?" Alison suggested.

"Seems so. Well, this strategy to raise taxes on tobacco was being planned for other states, too such as Colorado—your adopted state—but in order to avoid the same agency infighting and to launder the account, in 1991 along comes the Project called ASSIST from the Deparment of Health and Human Serivces, based on data from the National Cancer Institute, the NCI hired the Advocacy Foundation…"

Alison audibly sighed, and Rick could tell that she was becoming impatient.

"Now, wait, it gets better," he continued. "I also learned that these two organizations have worked together in the past on other projects…"

"What two organizations?" Alison asked.

"The National Cancer Institute and the Advocacy Foundation," Rick clarified, "so, like I was going to say, it must have been old-home week when the tax dollars started coming through the ASSIST program to the Advocacy Foundation."

"Wait, wait, wait—what's the Advocacy Foundation?" Alison asked.

"Well, the Advocacy Foundation is another nonprofit—ya know, tax-exempt organization—started in 1984 by two men who were, for years, lobbyists in Washington, D.C. Once the NCI established the ASSIST program—which, as you know, is an acronym for American Stop Smoking Intervention Study Program. Sounds innocent enough, doesn't it?" Rick asked rhetorically.

"No, I didn't know…and yes, very innocent."

"Anyway, these guys with the Advocacy Foundation were hired—oh, I must be politically correct and say they were 'awarded a grant'—by the National Cancer Institute, with tax dollars—to train and teach the staff of ASSIST and other staff from other volunteer health associations…basically, they were hired to teach them how to run a grassroots campaign.

"These two guys are really a piece of work, because, according to their own training survival guide, they actually ran 'media advocacy,' which was just their fancy label for legislative lobbying, otherwise known as political campaigns—nothing like the educational campaigns the National Cancer Institute was paying them for." Alison was reminded of the NCA's committee guidebooks at the meeting she attended at Connie's house. "But, like I said, those at the NCI must have turned a blind eye, because I think they knew exactly what was going on, and they knew they might get caught. So in order to avoid discovery and keep the tax dollars flowing to the Advocacy Foundation, the grants were laundered through another organization in Washington, who then paid the Advocacy Foundation for training services or workshops. Pretty slick, huh?"

"The Advocacy Foundation should have their tax-exempt status revoked, besides going to jail," shouted Alison into the phone.

"Hey, don't shoot the messenger," Rick patiently replied. "Ya want to hear the rest?"

"I'm sorry…I didn't mean to shout."

"You're forgiven," he said.

"Why did the NCI need these guys, anyway?" Alison questioned.

"There is a technique to Astroturfing, Alison," Rick said.

"Astroturfing?" she asked.

"You *have* been locked up in the lab too long," he said mockingly.

"Okay, okay," Alison said, "just tell me what Astroturfing is."

"It's a form of propaganda whose techniques usually consist of a few people attempting to give the impression that mass numbers are enthusiastically advocating some specific cause. The word is used to make reference to a false or artificial grassroots effort."

"Very clever," Alison said dryly, remembering Connie's remark about appearing to have a lot more people and the video Mitch showed of all the people marching.

"So, let me get this straight—a Federal agency set up a program, funded with taxpayer dollars, and the program's goal is to legislate an increase in state taxes on tobacco, while cloaked in the rhetoric of public health?"

"Yup."

"…and many of the staff from the…uh…voluntary health associations —were being trained with your tax dollars, too!"

"Now to bring it closer to home…or, rather, your *new* home," Rick said, qualifying his next remark. "Colorado was one of the states that bought into the ASSIST program. Of course, it was sold to states like Colorado as a means to get people to stop smoking. But the taxes were never allocated for helping the needy who already had cancer; the actual beneficiaries of this ASSIST program are the tax-exempt voluntary health associations—the VHAs—like the one that your friend Connie is working for. You see, Alison, these nonprofits cannot lobby for Federal funding without violating tax laws, but they *can* lobby legislation at the state level."

For a moment, Alison was speechless. Then, "How do you know all this is true?" she asked suspiciously. Then she added, "Of course, Rick, I would never doubt you—or your thoroughness, but what's your source?"

"You're right, most whistleblowers would be discouraged in disclosing any of this, out of fear of losing their jobs, being intimidated, or even retaliation by one of these national nonprofit organizations."

The words that Mitch spoke at the recruitment party came back to Alison, "…no one will believe you."

"I guess I can see that," she replied. "Who doesn't want to cure cancer…right?"

"Was that sarcasm I heard in your voice?" Rick said, and Alison could picture the grin on his face as he spoke; he knew her very well.

"If you're interested in reading a well-documented and well-written book by two very brave men who wrote on the subject, pick up Professor James T. Bennett's book, *Cancer Scam*..."

"Professor?" Alison asked.

"Yes, he's a professor of Economics at George Mason University. He wrote the book along with another professor, Thomas DiLorenzo, from Loyola College in Baltimore. I'm sure the nonprofit organizations they wrote about tried to intimidate both of them, but I also learned that the universities backed them," Rick said. "Oh...and by the way, there is some interesting reading about the ASSIST program in your adopted state of Colorado that you might want to read about, too."

"I've heard quite enough," Alison said, as all the information was swimming in her head. "I can't thank you enough, Rick. You've given me a lot to digest. I'll get the book as soon as I put down the phone."

"Well, I have to go, my dear," Rick said. "You just take care of yourself, and stay safe. We all miss you."

Alison could hear the sincerity in Rick's voice. Tears began to well up in her eyes as she said good-bye. She missed him, too. Maybe she missed him too much. Over the last few years, since Jack's death, Rick was someone she could always confide in. She missed those talks they used to have that were more like debates. Then, not wanting to dwell on the emptiness she felt at that moment, Alison put Dinah on her leash to take a long walk down by the river...to think.

As she walked down the bike trail, her thoughts became clearer. If what Rick said was true, her intuition was validated. The conduct of the National Cancer Association was not as ethical as they wanted people to believe...but still, Rick didn't mention any recent lawsuits, so that probably meant there weren't any laws broken—at least none that could be proven in a court of law. Still, the dissipation seemed intentional and deliberate, which was what made it all so unethical.

So, what should she do about it? She could tell Connie

what she learned and mention the book. "How would that help?" Alison thought to herself. No. She couldn't say anything to Connie—not now—not just before the fundraising event. That would absolutely destroy her, especially after she had worked so hard. "What could Connie do about it anyway?" Alison thought. If she backed out of the event, it would only hurt her reputation, which—in this small town—was so important. And the rumors Alison knew would start…no, she had to make it appear that Connie had nothing to do with any disclosure.

"Hmmm—I could write an exposé in the local paper, with the information from Professor Bennett's book," Alison said to Dinah as they walked. The dog looked back at Alison as if she understood. "No. Like Mitch said, no one would believe it—or want to believe it—even if the paper did publish my piece. I'm still the newcomer in town.

"What if, after these folks learned more about the unethical manipulation by the National Cancer Association, they still wanted to March at Night? Now, wouldn't that be absurd!" Alison thought. Then she remembered the video that Mitch played at the recruitment party and the people as they walked together arm in arm. Maybe, for some people, it wasn't about the money…maybe it was about that special night when everyone comes together in support of each other and to remember those who died of cancer. And maybe, for some of them, it was just about a big pajama party—and only about the party. Maybe some of the businesses donated money to become a sponsor just to advertise their business at the event. Or maybe it was just about looking like you care about a cure for cancer, even though they might not. Alison was now feeling very cynical. People volunteer for different reasons; she learned that while volunteering back in New Jersey, and she should remember that.

Deception in a Small Town

Alison thought that perhaps she was too quick to judge the people in her new home of Rosemont, so she decided to wait—wait until after the event; wait and be patient. But waiting was a hard thing for Alison to do.

❧ Chapter Sixteen ☙

The next morning, Alison stopped by the library to see if the book Rick had recommended was on the shelf. Not surprisingly, it wasn't listed...not even on interlibrary loan. *Cancer Scam* was published in 1998 and wouldn't be in any of the local bookstores. She decided to order it online and put a rush on it.

Three days later, it came in the mail. That evening, sitting in her study, Alison began reading. Everything Rick had said was detailed and documented.

"Professor Bennett really did his homework," Alison said to herself, impressed. "No wonder the National Cancer Association doesn't want people to read it. It also explains why the organization Professor Bennett wrote about tried to intimidate him," she thought.

One section in the book that Rick had referred to was regarding an event that happened in Colorado in 1986. On page 153, Alison read,

> ...in April of 1986, ACS-Colorado was given an endowment from the estate of Horase H. and Jeanette D Brooks valued at $3.3 million (the Brooks Trust). Under the Trust's terms, the funds could be used to erect and equip a building in Colorado or *in any other manner that the ACS-Colorado's Board of Directors designate.*

Deception in a Small Town

"If the health of the public in Colorado through early treatment and prevention was their mission, then why wasn't this money spent by the National Cancer Association, instead of them continuing to raise funds and ask for donations from the public?" Alison wondered.

She read on,

...Nothing was done with the money until December 1991 when the ACS-Colorado claimed that a court ruling was needed to interpret how the Trust might legitimately be spent. The fact that ACS-Colorado waited for five and half years to obtain such a ruling raises serious questions about the intent to use the Trust to fight cancer in Colorado.

"How many lives in rural Colorado could have been saved during those five years?" Alison asked herself. The mobile mammogram machine Connie and the hospital had asked for from the National Cancer Association would have been money well spent. How many lives could have been saved if cases of breast cancer and lung cancer had been detected earlier? How many people in Rosemont and other rural areas would still be walking around today—not just being remembered with ribbons and tears? If that money had been spent on a mobile mammogram machine for rural Colorado, how many more lives would have been saved?

Reading on, Alison learned,

The Denver Probate judge who heard the case noted that "the ACS has no present plans for utilizing the principal of the fund" and ruled that the Board of Directors of ACS-Colorado could use the Trust for any purpose that "will best promote the general purposes and work of the ACS." Tobacco education would have been an ideal use of the money, given to incessant antismoking campaign of the ACS.

Professor Bennett continued,

Two years later on January 9, 1993, the Board of the ACS-Colorado adopted a "position statement" on the Trust which states that the Colorado Division retains control of the funds in the Brooks Trust because of the uncertainty of the economy... The interest earned from the Brooks Trust should continue to be used to support the budget of the Colorado Division.

Alison was stunned. She looked at the references used in the book, then read Professor Bennett's analysis of the event:

> Thus, the primary beneficiaries of the Trust are the executives and staff of the …Colorado [division] who can count on a steady stream of income from the endowment. At the current spending rates, ACS-Colorado could operate with funds on hand for at lease three years without seeking additional donations from the public.

Skipping ahead to page 154, she found:

> As needy Coloradans suffer from cancer, an opportunity has been lost to put these assets to use in the battle against the disease. The lever of zeal and commitment from antismoking activists apparently depends on who pays for the advocacy. If taxpayers foot the bill, smoking is a critical issue; if the ACS's own funds are at stake, tobacco control must take a back seat to the comforts of ACS executives and staff.

Alison put the book down and stared out the window. She had come to the same conclusion as Professors Bennett and DiLorenzo. Dinah came over and put her head in Alison's lap, and she began stroking Dinah's head. "Oh, how I wish Jack was still alive," she told Dinah. "He would help me reason through this…. Should I or shouldn't I? Should I expose the fraud? If I don't say something or speak out about it, then I would be condoning the fraud."

But then, that little grinning smile sitting on Alison's left shoulder seemed to say, "Right, but it's not like the organization is breaking the law. It's none of your business, Alison." She ignored that whispering voice. She knew herself too well…and she couldn't live with inaction. There's something called "integrity," and Alison saw this in the people of Rosemont. It was what she admired in Connie.

Alison said softly to Dinah, "Besides, even if I do speak out, people will have to make their own choice to fundraise or be a volunteer. It must remain their choice. But if I don't speak out, then they will never have the option to choose with full knowledge…and they deserve to know. These are wonderful, generous people in Rosemont; they should be free to come to their own conclusions…make their own decisions. I'll only be exposing them to the facts They can deny the facts, but that's their choice, too. Each one of them will have to live with their decision…whatever it is."

Dinah had gotten up and gone to the back door. Alison noticed the digital clock on the video component read 11 p.m. She followed Dinah to the back porch, waited until she returned, then turned off the back porch light, locked the back door, and ascended the stairs. The thought of people choosing for themselves with full knowledge of the situation clinched it for her; she'd have to speak out.

But how was she to expose the fraud? That what the question that now shadowed Alison.

❧ Chapter Seventeen ☙

Over the next couple of weeks, Alison noticed posters in store windows advertising the March at Night fundraiser. Alison knew Connie was busy with her committees, but with only two weeks before the fundraiser, Connie seemed only to have time to wave to Alison over the back fence. One morning, a week before the event, Alison went over to see her, bringing some tomatoes she had just picked up at the farmers market. She had not made herself available to Connie and didn't want Connie to think she was avoiding her.

"Hi Connie, how's it going?" Alison asked as she held out the tomatoes. "I thought you would like these."

"Oh, aren't you a dear. Come on in, I was just folding and arranging the t-shirts by squad. We usually have too many smalls…and someone always complains."

"Oh, these are nice," Alison remarked as she fingered a pile of the folded t-shirts sitting on Connie's dining room table. "Did you get them printed locally?"

"Heavens, no," Connie said with a chuckle. "I couldn't even suggest it. The national logo for the NCA can't be used without authorization, and the art is commissioned on a national level. Every year the artwork is different…but it would be nice to keep the business local, wouldn't it?"

"Sure would be," Alison said. "What can I help you with?" she then asked, knowing there was always something to be done.

"Well, you can finish folding the t-shirts and bundling them by squad," Connie said. The two women worked in silence for a while. Alison was debating whether now was a good time to ask Connie the question she had been planning to ask. She wanted to know where Connie stood in general, on right and wrong. Feeling the time was right, she asked, "Connie, can I ask you a silly hypothetical question? Well, it's not really silly, but perhaps inappropriate, or maybe awkward…."

"Stop with the qualifications—if you want to ask a question, just ask," Connie said impatiently.

Over the past week, Alison had thought through this carefully to find out which side of an ethical question Connie would come down on. The answer would tell her much about Connie's character. Up to this moment, she had assumed Connie would answer as she hoped. Or would she?

"Okay," Alison continued. "If your husband was having an affair, would you want to know?"

Connie stopped what she was doing and looked up with a stare as big as a deer's eyes in headlights.

"What!?" Connie yelled incredulously.

"If your husband was having an affair…."

Connie cut off Alison, saying, "I heard you the first time. Why on God's green earth do you want to know that?"

"If you don't want to answer it, you don't have to," Alison said rather self-consciously. Connie studied Alison and seemed to realize how important an answer was to her.

"You're serious, aren't you?" she said, having no idea why the question was being asked. Perhaps because they were both widows?

"Yes," Alison said tentatively.

So rather than offering a flip answer, which was her style, Connie seemed to give the question thought before she spoke, and then answered, "Well, yes. I would want to know."

Alison was silent, allowing Connie to continue. "People aren't usually put in jail for having affairs, but it breaks the contract and the promises that two people enter into through marriage."

"So, even though it isn't against the law, you would want to know?"

"Yes."

"Why?" Alison asked for clarification.

"Because it's about trust. I have to trust the man I married, and he must trust me. That's more of what a marriage contract is about...I think."

"Trust? In what way?" Alison asked, now encouraged

"I would always have to trust that he is true to me...."

"In other words, 'truthful'?" Alison offered, blurting out the word.

"Yes, I suppose—truthful. That's what integrity and giving your word is all about," Connie said with a smile, as if she enjoyed this opportunity to visit her core values.

"Would you use the words 'unethical' or 'immoral' to describe an affair?" Alison now had to establish the distinction, so she probed further.

After a thoughtful pause, Connie replied, "Yes."

"Would you say that trust and the truth are part of any contract?" Alison asked, and at that moment, she thought of Jack and the contract law he once practiced.

"Hey, you said only one question," Connie replied. "I'm no lawyer."

Alison smiled with relief, "Perhaps not, but you are an honest person with integrity—and that's why I asked you a hypothetical question." She smiled again, and the two women went back to work and their own thoughts in the silence of Connie's front room.

ଔ Chapter Eighteen ଲ

Alison woke early the morning of the fundraiser, which was slightly overcast. Knowing she would be gone most of the day and that evening, she wanted to walk Dinah and stay as close to the usual routine as possible. Even when a radio was left on, Dinah would get nervous if the routine was broken. Connie knew Alison would have to leave the event from time to time to check on Dinah, and that was fine with her.

The forecast that week had been for wind with afternoon thunderstorms. Connie had concerns about the weather during the event, but there wasn't much that could be done. She and Alison had called all the squad leaders the night before and told them to remind their members to bring rain gear, just in case.

Alison had arranged to be at Connie's house around 9 o'clock. She drove out of her drive and around the corner to back into her neighbor's driveway. They would need both cars to bring all the tables, chairs, and tents stored in Connie's garage to the high school athletic field, the venue for the event. Connie was in a flippant mood.

Curious, Alison commented, "You're in a good mood…"

"Why not?" Connie offered. "I will get to see a lot of folks from town, and there isn't much I can do about anything at this point. I have a saying, 'It is what it is.' So, now I just try and enjoy the closeness of the community."

Deception in a Small Town

Alison smiled to herself. One of things she liked about Connie was her practical perspective of the moment. Once both cars were loaded, Alison followed Connie to the high school.

Cars were already arriving, and Bert, the grounds maintenance supervisor for the high school—now the facility committee chairperson for the event—was directing participants pulling trolleys and dollies onto the field. There were tents to be put up, electrical generators to bring in, port-a-potties to offload, and barbeques to fire up. She was still wondering how this all cured cancer.

The two women pulled up to the entrance to the athletic field and began emptying the contents of both SUVs stacking things against the fence that surrounded the dirt track. It seemed quite the carnival atmosphere to Alison as she surveyed the field. She waited by the boxes and tables until Connie told her where to put them.

After each trip from the cars, Alison watched the chaos as some members of a few squads started small squabbles over their designated location at the edge of the field. There were 13 spots for the 13 expected squads signed up for the event. All the locations had to be near the track at the edge of the grass field. She understood that there would have to be enough room for everyone to have a chair or small tent for resting during the evening's event; and with over 150 people, the field was big enough. As well, there was extra room needed if a squad chose to sell food items at the event, raising more money. The women would be selling breads and cakes, and the men—not as numerous as the women, usually dragged along to the event by their wives—were manning large open BBQs. All the money raised would go to the NCA...which, Alison was told, encouraged competition among the squads.

Alison was fascinated by all this unsupervised interaction. She thought about Mitch Cutter, how this seemingly disorganized set-up must drive him as mad as a hatter. She pictured

Mitch in her mind, riding a little motor scooter like a clown in the circus, putting around the field and fussing more efficiently. Alison smiled to herself. She wondered when he would show up, along with the others from the NCA.

She remembered Connie saying that not everyone shows up.

"Sometimes people have a work-shift change, or a child will get sick and the parents, who are part of a squad, stay home. There can be all sorts of reasons...," and Connie had added, "...none of which are good enough for the NCA. Last year, Mitch and Marcia had a fit because one of the squads dropped out at the last minute. This year, the hospital squad decided not to come because of the uncertainty of their schedule. You just never know until that night, and also we have to allow for stragglers who aren't signed up but come anyway for the BBQ." Connie's "what is" philosophy came to mind. "I kinda like that openness about the event—it's become more of a community happening, and even though the NCA frowns on the drop-ins, I like it!" she said.

Now, as the two women were standing there in the middle of the field, a man dressed as a fly-fisherman walked by. Alison thought, "That's odd. How very lost this poor man looks." Then, as he passed her, she saw the sign on his back that read, "Fishing for a cure."

Connie smiled at Alison, "Oh, you'll see others dressed in costumes, too." At that moment a person—Alison couldn't tell if it was a man or a woman—walked by dressed as Groucho Marx. The sign on his back read, "Cancer is no joke."

Alison learned that all the squads had the option of dressing up for the event, but most just wore the t-shirt over a pair of blue jeans as they set up their tents and established their territory. Perhaps Alison was the only one who saw the ironic humor in this grassroots events being held on a field of "turf." "Oh, well," she thought, "I'll just keep it to myself."

Deception in a Small Town

The bleachers at the athletic field were only 20 rows up and could probably only seat 300 people. Alison learned they were used for seating for the participants and visitors during the long event.

Alison continued to follow Connie around like a Girl Friday, "Which is appropriate," she thought to herself, since it was a Friday in late July. She helped Connie set up tents and tables, banners and booths. When they got to the Advocacy booth, Alison paused. She was curious to know what Connie thought the NCA's advocacy purpose was, so she questioned her about it.

"Oh, this booth is mandatory for the event," was Connie's answer. "It's some political lobbying organization. Politics is not my thing. Mitch knows this, so he brings in a staff member from the Front Range to man the booth. Most folks here want their money to go to cancer research, not politics. Here, I'll introduce you," Connie said, grabbing Alison's arm and pulling her toward the booth. The man at the Advocacy booth spotted Connie and came out from behind the table to greet her. This gave Alison an opportunity to size him up. He was a tall, slim man, clean shaven with short-trimmed hair. The graying at his temples made him, Alison thought, middle-aged. He was dressed in an expensive Pal Zileri linen knit shirt, beige Valentini cotton trousers, and a pair of calfskin Martin Dingman loafers. He had that "Wall Street" look—that's what Alison called these corporate guys whose success was measured by power and status, not achievement or character. After 20 years in the pharmaceutical business, she knew the type; knew that, in most cases, this kind of expensive packaging was used to distract from its content.

Connie introduced Alison, then hurried off leaving the two of them standing together. Mr. Wall Street asked Alison, "Would you like to sign up as a member of GALO?"

"Sorry, I don't drink," Alison politely lied. Mr. Wall Street smiled and said, with a condescending smirk, "No…no. Not the wine company. This is the national advocacy arm of the NCA. GALO is an acronym for Grassroots Advocacy Lobby Organization." He said it slowly, pronouncing each word carefully as if Alison was feeble minded.

"Oh, thank you for that explanation," was the only thing Alison could think of to say. "Like most bureaucratic agencies, they sure like their acronyms," she thought. Then, collecting her wits, she asked, "Tell me, what do you do for GALO? And if I join, where does my money go?"

With these two questions asked, Alison was curious which he would choose to answer. She knew that if he chose the first question, that would confirm he was a self-absorbed jerk. If he answered the second question, then she just might learn something.

He chose to answer neither. "Well, the organization is only a few years old...."

"Oh, really," Alison said. "When was it started?" she asked curiously, instinctively searching for another piece of the puzzle. She remembered that, according to Rick, Prop 99 was on the California ballot in 1988. The ASSIST program was enacted in 1991, and Professor Bennett's book was written in 1998.... Alison was looking for a pattern.

"It was established in 2001 and is a nonprofit organization. It's all right here in the brochure...," and with much indifference, Mr. Wall Street handed Alison a pamphlet from one of the stacks lying on the table. "Here it says...let's see...oh, yes—your money goes to fund grassroots lobbying and media campaigns to make every state smoke-free and to increase tobacco taxes and funding for cancer research."

Alison realized this was what Rick was saying when he told her about Proposition 99 in California, and what Professor Bennett wrote about in his book, *Cancer Scam*. It also supported what she had read about the National Institute of Health's ASSIST program.

Deception in a Small Town

Mr. Wall Street continued, "The money also goes to provide brochures directly to the public and to support training workshops for volunteers and staff members, so we can strengthen the lobbying movement in Washington, D.C. We try to influence government policy on a Federal level," Mr. Wall Street said with arrogant pride. The Advocacy Foundation instantly came to Alison's mind, and how taxpayer dollars are funneled to such organizations.

"You want to find a cure for cancer, don't you?" Mr. Wall Street asked.

"Well...of course," Alison said.

"Then sign here...membership is fifteen dollars...but you can, of course, donate more."

"Is my donation tax deductible?" Alison asked. Having read Professor Bennett's book, she already knew the answer, but didn't want Mr. Wall Street to know she knew.

"It *is* a nonprofit organization...what do you think?"

"How evasive," Alison thought. She knew this organization wasn't a 501-C3. According to the brochure, it was a 501-C4, and donations are *not* tax deductible.

"It's not a matter of what I think...I'm *asking* you," Alison said as non-confrontationally as she could, while still staying direct.

"Uh, what do you mean? It's a nonprofit organization, and we would like you to think we do good work. We need to influence state and Federal legislation to help cure cancer...that's all I'm saying. It's all right here in the brochure...."

Now, in the most condescending way, he continued, "Do you want to cure cancer? If so, join GALO."

"No, thank you," Alison said politely. She never seemed to get straight answers from anyone associated with the NCA. But she knew that no politician had ever donned a lab coat, or passed a law that directly helped a cancer patient without a self-serving motive.

"Politicians are in the business of getting reelected, and if they can work through such organizations as GALO to rally positive public relations for their own reelection campaign, then they will," Alison said to Mr. Wall Street.

Walking off, she was thinking, "What an arrogant, pompous, self-absorbed political hack!" Alison knew this was no way to make friends, but she resented his even being at the event. It seemed that somehow politics jaded the sincere motives of the good people of Rosemont. Then she added to herself, "Calm down, Alison. You need to find Connie."

She decided not to tell her friend about her conversation with Mr. Wall Street...at least not until after the event.

Once she located Connie, Alison said, with a forced smile, "You were right about politics...."

Then together, they opened one of the boxes marked "Made in China" that had been stored in Connie's garage. Inside were bundles of large aqua-colored satiny ribbons. The ribbons were about two feet long and eight inches wide and made of soft plastic. Each was attached to a three foot long, very thin balsawood stick, making the ribbon appear like a mini flag or banner. Each of these had the NCA logo on it and a long line on which someone could write something. There were a few bunches of big fluorescent, felt-tip waterproof pens bundled together with a rubber band at the bottom of the box. Alison wondered about all of this.

"What are these for?" she asked Connie. She pulled a sign from the same box that read, "Ribbon Runners, $5.00."

"Well, these ribbons are for people to write the names of their loved ones on, whoever they want to be remembered at tonight's event—like someone who is suffering from cancer or who has died from cancer. I always buy one and put John's name on it," Connie said.

"So...that's what the pens are for," Alison deduced.

"Smart lady," Connie replied sarcastically. "Then the ribbons are stuck in the grass at the edge of the track—sort of like little flags—with names on all of them. All night long they flutter in the breeze—they look really cool when a lot of them are all lining the track and blowing in the breeze.

"I remember one year when we couldn't place them out on the track because of the rain and wind, but I don't think that will be a problem this year," Connie said. "Oh, and by the way, this is where I'd like you to work for the first few hours of the event—is that okay?" she asked Alison.

Alison said nothing, considering the job.

"Really, it's an easy job—and best of all, you can see the whole show from here—best seat in the house!" Connie encouraged with a smile.

"Well, in that case....sure, I'll work the ribbon runners for you. Just please don't forget I'm here, because you know I'll have to leave to let Dinah out, okay?" Alison said.

"Yes, of course, but," Connie hesitated. Then a very serious look came over her face. "I hope this doesn't sound too odd," she paused.

"Hey, remember you're talking to the hypothetical question lady—*now* who's qualifying!" Alison said jokingly.

"Yeah, you're sure right about that!" Connie said, letting out a good laugh. "Okay, uhh...please don't use the words 'cost' or 'sale' or 'purchase' to anyone who wants a ribbon. Just use the word 'donate'—just say, 'We're asking for a donation of five dollars for a ribbon,' okay?"

"Can I take less?" Alison asked.

"Ya, you sort'a have to...." Then Connie began to explain her request. "Ya see, we're not supposed to sell the ribbons, because then March at Night is profiting from the misfortune, illness, or death of the people in our community. All these types of events in this rural part of Colorado are competing for prizes and gifts that are based on which community raises the most money. So if we start selling the ribbons for people who have died of cancer, then the event will be benefiting from a cancer death.

"It's a technical point...and from the look on your face, you seem to have grasped its significance," Connie said, smiling at Alison.

"Yes!" Alison said. She was incredulous. *She* thought the aim of the NCA was to save lives, not profit from peoples' deaths...and prevent cancer with early detection, not benefit from those suffering with cancer. Everything here was reversed and turned backwards. It was like being in the house of mirrors at Coney Island. What was left was right and what was right was left; what should be right was wrong, and what was good was distorted. Alison thought the whole thing absurd.

"Oh, one more thing," Connie said as she arranged the ribbons on the table, "I know you've never met any of the executives or trainers from the NCA office in Denver, but sometimes the regional office seeds the event with spies. I really shouldn't say that...," she confided. "We're told they're here to make sure the event is run according to the Federal laws for 501-C3, but they've been known to bother some of the participants and question—or, rather, *interrogate*—some of the committee chairpersons. But ya want to know what I think?" Connie added in a quiet covert tone. "Sure!" Alison said with hushed enthusiasm.

"I think they just like to get out of the office, rent a big Escalade for the weekend, and come over here for a good steak and some fly-fishing." Then Connie winked at Alison and they both started laughing.

"On a more serious note—they will probably visit your table, because you're new with the event. Just be prepared," Connie added. Then before Alison had time to ask another question, Bert rushed up to the table looking very upset. He pulled Connie to one side, spoke quietly in her ear, and they both hurried away. Now Alison didn't know what to think. Was all this true, or was it just Connie's cynical nature? She hoped it was the latter.

On Connie's way back by Alison's table, Alison asked—as if everything was perfectly normal—"What do I do with the money? Do I take checks? What about credit cards?"

"Cash is preferred…then checks. We're not set up to run credit cards, even though Marcia wishes we could," Connie replied. "If you have to leave, just take the cash box over to Marge at squad check-in…ya, that'll work well. I'll make sure someone comes to relieve you around five, so you can get home and back by 6 p.m. for the opening ceremony."

Then Alison turned around to see a woman standing in front of her table. She wanted a ribbon: It had started.

⊱ Chapter Nineteen ⊰

Shortly before 5 p.m., most of the tents were up and the loudspeaker was being tested. Alison was busy at her booth, when Connie rushed up to the ribbon-running table to see how she was doing.

"I'm sorry…I'm sorry, but I don't have anyone to relieve you. I'll stay…you just go home and let Dinah out," Connie hurriedly said. Alison sensed an uneasiness building in Connie as she scanned the field, offering Alison a distracted, forced smile.

"Calm down, it's okay…I can wait. Dinah has her doggie door and I left the back porch light on when I left. She'll be okay. But thanks for checking on me," Alison said. Connie offered a grateful sigh and rushed off.

Beyond the clatter of busyness around her table, Alison noticed a group of well-dressed men and women all standing together near the entrance to the field. She counted six. Then she heard Mitch Cutter's annoying laughter coming from the same direction. That identifiable laugh caused her to more carefully focus on the seemingly anxious group. Alison saw Mitch standing among the group by the NCA Advocacy table that included Mr. Wall Street. Her view became blocked by all the people who were in front of her table, so Alison tried to peer around them; she wanted to watch the group of six. Impatiently, she got up from behind the table to get a better view. Using an excuse to not seem so obvious, she reminded everyone, "Return the fluorescent felt pens after writing your names," and all the while she watched the group at the Advocacy table.

Soon, a large gold-colored, four-door Cadillac Escalade pulled up to the gate in front of the field. A short stocky man got out of the back seat and hurriedly went to the passenger side of the car, opening the door. Out stepped a very tall, slender, dark-haired woman. She looked out over the event as if waiting to be noticed by her subjects, the mingling crowd. She took a few steps and the short stocky man closed the car door. Then the gold SUV drove away. The tall dark-haired woman walked over to the waiting well-dressed group of six, followed hurriedly by the short stocky man who had to take two steps to every one of hers. Alison watched as the group of six all gathered around the woman, shaking her hand and humbly bowing as though she was some sort of a potentate.

Alison recognized Marcia Harris standing with Mitch Cutter. She was still dressed cheaply and needed to comb her hair. Alison noticed she was wearing two-inch, aqua-colored stilettos. "The silliest thing to ever wear to an event such as this," Alison thought. "The only thing this woman is good for in those shoes is aerating the turf!"

Alison now could make out the others in the group of six. There was Alan Gross, Mr. Wall Street, Mitch, and Marcia all standing around the tall dark-haired woman. She noticed Mitch talking with Mr. Wall Street, then the two men looked over toward her at the ribbon-running table. Alison saw their glance and ignored them. She watched as the tall dark-haired woman and her procession of followers began to walk onto the grassy field. The group stopped by a few of the booths, then they headed her way, stopping in front of Alison's booth. Alison, now seated back behind the table, looked up. The tall dark-haired woman was standing over the table, scrutinizing Alison. She stood up from her chair to meet the woman who was now so close that Alison could see how old and haggard she looked. Her black beady eyes were sunken into a drawn face that seemed stretched over high bony cheeks. "Perhaps too many face-lifts," Alison thought as she studied the woman further. Her hair was jet black, with no warm brown highlights—just black as coal. She was dressed all in black, as well: black slacks, black shoes, and a tight-fitting black tunic top that hung out over her slacks. The woman wore one piece of jewelry. It was a long gaudy necklace of very large blood-red irregular beads the size of golf balls, strung onto a thin sterling silver chain that hung around her thin wrinkled neck. The string of red baubles fell between her two tiny breasts. The beads reminded Alison of small shrunken heads that a shaman would wear as a fetish.

"Very curious," Alison thought to herself as she smiled politely at the woman. The woman, ignoring Alison, began to smooth the front of her tight-fitting black satin tunic top. Her hand traveled down her front, and she glanced around to see if the men in her entourage were noticing the gesture.

"...and what is your name, dearie?" she asked Alison.

"My name is Alison," she replied with a smile, holding out her hand to shake.

The woman refused the gesture. In that momentary pause, Alison pulled her hand back and asked, "And what's yours—*dearie*?" She emphasized the last word. There were a few giggles heard, and the woman's face turned crimson.

"Oh, how nice," Alison thought to herself. "Now her face matches the beads...what if they *are* truly shrunken heads?" She wasn't sure if the woman was outraged or simply embarrassed, but she didn't much care.

"Idiot!" shouted the woman, looking at Alison. The short stocky man who was standing next to her now anxiously tugged on her sleeve. The woman bent down so he could whisper something in her ear. Then she stood straight and—noticing people were now watching the exchange—she looked down at Alison with her piercing black eyes and said, with a clenched jaw and a phony smile, "You must be *new*."

"Yes, I am," Alison said. "I'm new to this event, new to Rosemont, and new to Colorado. I'm sorry, but perhaps your reputation has not reached the East Coast," she said sarcastically. "I still don't know who *you* are." There was some laughter from the crowd that was now gathered.

"Silence!" the woman shouted, holding her palm out like a traffic cop. Then she spoke again, "I am Juanita Montoya, the Executive Vice President of the Colorado Division of the National Cancer Association."

"Well, welcome to the Rosemont March at Night event," Alison said with a smile. "Would you like to donate for a ribbon?"

The tall dark-haired woman did not answer, but instead turned abruptly and walked away. Then, from somewhere in the back of the crowd, a subdued applause was heard. Alison searched for its source…but then it was gone.

After the woman left Alison's booth, followed by her cortege, Connie appeared—almost from nowhere.

"Is she gone? I really dislike that woman," Connie said.

"Where'd you come from?" Alison asked. "Were you trying to avoid her? Did you hear any of that?"

"Yes, to both questions. I sure wish I could be that fearless," Connie said. "You can get away with it once, but she'll have your head if you ever stand up to her again."

Connie's remark about "have your head" made Alison think of the woman's necklace. Maybe those beads really *were* shrunken heads from past volunteers who had crossed Juanita Montoya!

Then she replied, "Thanks for the warning."

"Hey, the opening ceremony is about to start," Connie said. "Come on…"

Alison locked the cash box and, with it tucked under her arm, joined Connie closer to the track. The participants were gathering at one end of the field; the fast-beat music began to blast out from the field's PA system. Mitch was at the microphone that stood on the makeshift stage located under the scoreboard. He began to tap it.

"Testing…testing… "Welcome to the annual March at Night fundraiser. We are all here to find a cure for cancer…hope for a cure…let's make our dollar goal…."Alison, hearing this, thought, "What a silly thing to say." Mitch continued with the same rhetoric and cliché phrases he had spouted at the Recruitment Rally, and then—just like at the rally—he introduced Marcia. She had a difficult time walking up to the microphone in her aqua stilettos. With every other step, one of her heels would sink into the soft turf, and she would be jerked back until the heel of her shoe released. She looked ridiculous. A few of the people in the crowd that had gathered in front of the small stage started to snicker.

Finally arriving at the stage, she took the microphone from Mitch as he stepped off and stood back with the Executive Vice President's entourage, which was now standing next to the stage.

"Hi, y'aall…*soooo* good to see y'all agin! Today we have the honor of Juanita Montoya's presence with us, and—as y'all recall—she is our Executive Vice President of the Colorado Division of the National Cancer Association." Marcia began clapping her hands into the microphone, encouraging the crowd to applaud. Juanita Montoya offered a small royal wave to the crowd as if she was acknowledging her subjects. "As y'all know, Ms. Montoya's time is very valuable, and Rosemont should appreciate this great honor in being selected to have her company at your little ol' event. We all know how much your community depends on the National Cancer Association to help bring y'all this yearly event, and we all know that without the National Cancer Association, your little community would never have the slightest idea what to do or how to have such a splendid little ol' community event. Your community should be *soooo* very grateful to the National Cancer Association!"

Marcia paused, hoping for some applause that only came from the direction in which Mitch and the others were standing. "And how do you show your gratitude?" Marcia went on. "Y'all show that gratitude by raising as much money as y'all can for the National Cancer Association! Yea! Yea!" She started to jump up and down and clap loudly into the microphone while Juanita Montoya and her entourage looked on approvingly.

As Alison stood there watching this patronizing show, which seemed to be for the benefit of the staff from the National Cancer Association and had nothing to do with the mission of the organization, she thought that this whole event was nothing more than a symbolic display of pompous ceremony. But, knowing her predilection towards hasty conclusions, she paused and thought she should wait and see what came next—and to prove herself correct, of course!

Marge was on the track now, and people in aqua-colored t-shirts started to gather round her. They seemed to be coming from tents and out of chairs and simply appearing on the track.

"Stay with your squad…stay with your squad," Marge was shouting repeatedly to the growing confusion around her.

Then a starter's gun went off and Mitch shouted into the microphone, "Begin the march to cure cancer!" The music started and Marge, pumping her arms like the leader of a band, led the chaotic crowd down the track all dressed in aqua-colored shirts. As they passed in front of the bleachers, aqua and white balloons came floating up from behind the stands and rose into the evening sky.

"What pageantry!" thought Alison. "Connie was right…this *is* the best seat in the house!" Now looking around for her friend, she noticed Connie had joined the others on the track. Alison stood there alone as all the community of Rosemont passed in front of her. A crowd that numbered almost 200 continued to walk around the quarter-mile track, music blasting an upbeat tune. Like letting out a coil of ribbon, the cluster of chaos now began to stretch and thin. Not everyone in the crowd could keep up with Marge, and smaller, slower groups started to form and break off from the main body of marchers. Some people had locked arms together and others walked slowly, just holding hands. "This is quite a community," Alison smiled to herself.

Once Marge made it back to where she started, Mitch went up to the microphone and announced that hot dogs, hamburgers, and locally grown corn-on-the-cob were being served. He jumped from the stage and hurried over to be the first in line for the burgers. A few small groups stayed on the track and continued to march, but most left, forming another line behind Mitch in front of the BBQ booth.

Alison watched with interest. She was hungry but didn't want to stand in line, so she got up and decided to join some of the marchers. She took the cash box over to the sign-in table and gave it to Libby, the finance committee chairperson, then started onto the dirt track. Walking always cleared her mind.

Alison noticed people whose faces she had seen at the feed store, the grocery store, and the gas station. Most were into their own conversations and didn't even notice her. Time passed, and she began walking next to two other women, both younger that she.

"Hi," Alison said, hoping to be invited to walk with them. The two women smiled back, saying, "Please join us. We know you're new in town—we're friends of Connie's, too."

"Oh, how nice—thank you," Alison said. This would give her a chance to get to know some of the other women in town... That's why she was here, wasn't it?

"My name is Ruth. My husband is Ron—your realtor, I believe...?" the woman said, looking for recognition from Alison.

"Oh yes, of course," Alison said. "He was just great...did a wonderful job for me finding my house, and his staff was so helpful. What a great guy. Did he happen to mention that I would like to have you both over for a thank-you dinner soon? I could show you what I've done with the house."

"Yes, he did mention that, but with the kids and their sports, it's hard to plan. Once this march is over, we'll have more time."

"Oh, do you do this just for Connie, because she's running it?" Alison asked.

"Yes, and because my father died of lung cancer ten years ago. Our kids never really got to know him. I regret that," Ruth said, smiling at Alison. She was a pleasant woman in her late thirties, Alison thought. A short blonde pageboy haircut framed her round pink, full-cheeked face and blue eyes. She was someone you wouldn't notice unless you knew her.

"And I'm Janet," the other woman said, "Jimmy's mom?" again waiting for Alison to register the name.

"Oh, Jimmy. What a great kid...and a hard worker. He sure does a good job on my lawn, and he sure gets along with my dog, Dinah." Alison was happy to meet both these woman.

"How long have you had your dog?" Janet asked.

"Three years. I found her a year after my husband died"

"Yes, we're sorry. Connie told us you were a widow. Ya know, Connie is a great person. She'll be the first to help a neighbor, support a friend, or organize a fundraiser."

"Yes, she's a wonderful person, I'm finding out," Alison said sincerely, glad the conversation had moved from her dog and deceased husband. "She certainly did a fine job with this program," she said, referring to the evening's event.

"Did you know she's also involved with our local nonprofit that helps women with breast cancer?" Janet said.

"No, I didn't," Alison said with surprise.

"Oh yes—four years ago, when I got breast cancer, it was almost missed, but when I felt a lump, Connie insisted on driving me to Fremont for a mammogram. She also arranged transportation to and from the chemotherapy treatment after the cancer was discovered."

"How nice of her. Were you married?" Alison asked, hoping that didn't sound too blunt, and thinking that if Jack was alive, he would have wanted to be there, if it had been Alison with breast cancer.

"Oh yes…and I still am," Janet said with a smile that told Alison she wasn't taken aback by her bluntness. "But Josh was overseas in Afghanistan. And Jimmy, as you know, was just a kid; nine years old. The community was all I had for support, and the charge was led by Connie."

"What about Social Services or the National Cancer Association?" Alison asked.

"This is rural Colorado; we don't have the sophisticated services they offer in big cities. And we sure didn't have any National Cancer Association to help. I remember it was when I was going through my chemotherapy and traveling to Fremont that Connie went into their office and asked the National Cancer Association for support services in our community. Before her visit to their office in Fremont, the National Cancer Association had no interest in Rosemont. But after Connie's visit, they told her that if she started one of their annual fundraisers, they would help our community by bringing us some of their programs…"

"I heard you're still waiting."

"Yup. We still are.... Anyway, I help Connie with this fundraiser, because she still believes they'll keep their promise—and I believe in Connie."

"That's very noble," Alison said, hoping she didn't sound sarcastic.

"Anyway, Jimmy is the one who had it the worst," Janet continued, "and Connie was the first to notice that, too. I hope I'm not making Connie sound like a busybody—ya know, getting involved in everyone's business. It's just that, as a teacher, it was part of her job to let us parents know if kids seem to have emotional problems in school," Janet said.

"Oh, no—not at all. Tell me how Connie helped Jimmy…he seems fine," Alison replied reassuringly.

"Well, Jimmy was nine, and Josh had just gone off to war. I had just been diagnosed with cancer and, once chemo started, I was so tired and slept most of the day. Connie was Jimmy's fourth grade teacher, and she noticed him becoming withdrawn. He didn't participate in school activities and his grades started dropping off. On one of the drives to Fremont for chemo, she told me about it, and made the suggestion."

"What suggestion?" Alison prompted.

"Camp Good Grief. Connie suggested Jimmy go to Camp Good Grief," Janet acknowledged with a smile.

"Camp Good Grief?" Alison asked.

"Yes. Jimmy really didn't qualify, but Connie got him in."

"I'm sorry, I don't know what Camp Good Grief is," Alison said apologetically.

"Of course you don't; it's a local program. Camp Good Grief is run out of our local Hospice office here in Rosemont. It's for kids who've lost parents or siblings—some by accidents, some by illness. Every summer the program lasts a few days and is held at the church camp up in the foothills. The kids camp out, sing songs around a campfire, and talk to other kids in their same situation. Jimmy doesn't have any brothers or sisters, so being with kids his own age was really important, and he hadn't lost a parent—that's why he didn't qualify."

"Are they supervised?" Alison asked bluntly, and then thought it a stupid question.

"Oh, please—it's not a reality show!" Janet countered, which drew a chuckle from both Janet and Ruth. "Of course they're supervised—that's the best part. There are professional counselors there who're trained to help the kids express their feelings. It turned out that Jimmy was afraid of being abandoned. He had heard stories at school of people dying in wars and thought he might lose his dad, and he heard just as many stories that cancer kills. He saw me lose my hair, get very thin, and sleep all the time. I must have looked dead to him!" Janet said reflectively. "So you see, he thought he might be abandoned, and he was very scared. Once the counselors drew this out of him, they were able to discuss it with him, and with me. Without that Hospice program, who knows what would have happened to Jimmy. It was a godsend."

"Well, that sounds like a wonderful program. You're family sure had the community's support." Alison said thoughtfully "You truly are blessed to have such wonderful friends."

"Well, that's what neighbors do…if you need a hand, they pitch in," Janet said. The three women continued together around the track in silence, lost in their own thoughts.

As they came up to the start of the squad stations, Ruth was first to leave as she neared her squad's tent area. The women separated, saying good-bye. Alison then said to Janet, "If you happen to see Connie, please tell her I left for a moment to check on my dog, will you?"

"You bet," Janet replied. "I enjoyed chatting."

"Me, too," Alison smiled.

Alison continued walking, still deep in thought and the

night's stillness. She came upon another woman who was standing near one of the ribbon runners with her head bowed. She held a photograph in her hand. Alison stopped next to her and smiled respectfully.

"Someone very special?" Alison asked.

"Yes, my sister," came the reply. "The summer before she died, we walked together…she was fighting cancer at the time. It was a very special time for us," the woman said as she held out the photograph for Alison to see. Alison took the photograph. Even though she could hardly make out the figures in the dimming twilight, she answered, saying, "Yes, I can see why this event is so special to you. What kind of cancer did she die of?"

"Breast cancer…it runs in the family," the woman said.

"Oh, I'm so sorry…have you been genetically tested yet for the disease?" Alison asked, trying to sound sympathetic. The woman didn't answer. Alison knew that most cases of familial breast cancer were caused by either of two autosomal dominant genes, BRCA1 and BRCA2. The two genes were responsible for only around 5% of breast cancer cases, but if this woman's sister died of the genetic form of breast cancer, Alison knew that this woman had a 60% to 80% risk of developing the same kind in her lifetime. And if a mother or sister was diagnosed with breast cancer, the risk of a hereditary BRCA1 or BRCA2 gene mutation was about two-fold higher than in those women without a familial history. Alison realized this woman was at very high risk for developing the same kind of cancer that her sister died of.

Alison handed the photo back to the woman and continued speaking softly. "Did you know that there's a commercial test available to find out what your chances are for developing the same breast cancer your sister had? …it's been around since at least 2004."

"Yeah, the doctors told me about some kind of test," the woman sniffled, taking the photo back from Alison. "But those tests are very expensive, and our family doesn't have that kind of money."

"Gee, I'm so sorry…that's too bad," Alison replied. "Ya know, you really should be tested," she softly insisted. "I was thinking…"Alison said hesitately, concerned that perhaps she might be intruding into this woman's space—into her moment of remembrance—but she had to try. "Are you part of one of the squads marching tonight?"

"Yes…so?"

"May I ask …how much money did your squad raise for this event?"

"How much money…what?" the woman repeated as she looked up from the photo at Alison. Alison only smiled.

"Perhaps enough for that genetic testing?" Alison said, planting the thought in her mind. "Or better yet—perhaps the National Cancer Association will offer the genetic testing at our Cancer Center?" The woman said nothing. Alison just smiled, "Your sister was a lovely woman."

"Thank you," she said, looking down at the photo again. Alison continued walking, leaving the grieving woman standing as she had found her.

Alison was baffled: How can these wonderful people ignore their own health and future as well as that of their families because of an expensive test, yet choose to raise thousands of dollars for an organization that has no intention of helping them? She was still hoping it was the community celebration that brought them together, not the competitive fundraising; if they only knew what all their hard work and money went for…!

"These people are hoping for services that the National Cancer Association promised…three years and they're *still* waiting," thought Alison. "Yet, they have found ways to fill those needs themselves through their local churches and by starting small nonprofit community groups like Bosom Buddies and the local Hospice. I'll bet if these tenacious people could figure out a way to open their own cancer research lab, they would. They don't need the National Cancer Association—the National Cancer Association needs them!" Alison knew that the NCA, like most nonprofit organizations, was based on volunteers from local communities. So it's the volunteers' time, the volunteers' money, and the volunteers' contacts with their local community leaders, newspapers, and businesses that the nonprofits need. The NCA like most nonprofits would be nothing without the volunteers.

"Don't these folks know how important they are?" she thought. "Without them, the NCA would collapse like a house of cards!

"If volunteers only realized how much power they really have...if they could only be made to understand that," Alison thought to herself. She still held the conviction that these good-hearted people needed to be told the truth. As she walked, Alison became keenly aware of the still night. The winds that had been blowing during sunset now seemed to rest quietly under the stars. The smell of fresh-cut hay drifted on the cool waves of night air, and a symphony of sound from the crickets faded in and out from the hills above the high school athletic field. Again, Alison was glad she had moved here. Then as she left the track and walked to her car, she checked her watch: It was 10:45 p.m.

The porch light was on when Alison arrived home, and Dinah greeted her at the front door. After locking the doggie door and giving the Dobie a few biscuits, she was back out the door—back to the event. All was well.

When Alison returned to the track around 11:30, she noticed a commotion near the front gate. Some of the floodlights had now been turned on at that end of the field. It seemed a group had gathered. As she neared the area, she recognized Mitch standing with the Wall Street man; next to them was the short stocky man with Juanita Montoya. Alan Gross and Marcia were there, too. Connie and some of the other committee chairs were mingling in their own group to the side.

"That's odd," Alison said to herself. "I hope no one fell ill. I wonder what's happened?"

As she approached, Mitch began to jump up and down and, pointing at Alison, he hollered, "There she is! There she is!" Everyone assembled turned to look at her.

"Oh, dear me," Alison said. "What have I done?" Connie hurriedly rushed up to her and said, "There's some money missing. Don't say anything."

"Why not? I didn't steal it…why can't I try and help find it?"

At that moment, the two women were approached by the short stocky man. The man rudely stepped in front of Connie, pushing her back behind him. He looked determined. Alison and the short stocky man were face to face. His cynister eyes, that never blinked, stayed focused on Alison like a snake before it strikes. He grinned at Alison but said nothing. Now, the crowd began to gather around them. The man waited until Mitch, Marcia, the Wall Street man, and Juanita Montoya were all standing behind him. The group was silent; staring at Alison and the short stocky man, waiting to hear what would come next. Alison, realizing the maneuvering going on, concluded that they were trying to lay blame.

Not wanting to be on the defense, Alison initiated the first question, asking the man, "You seem to be upset… Is everything all right? Why don't you calm down and tell me what's going on," she said with a smile to the man. He ignored Alison's question, but those crowded around her seemed to sense her attempt to calm the situation. But he just stared at her with a glaring grin. Then he cleared his throat and in a voice, that all could hear, loudly asked,

"You were in charge of the ribbon-running booth, were you not?"

"So that's what it's about," Alison thought to herself. Alison knew to answer carefully.

"Well, actually, I'm not really the chairperson. In fact, I'm not sure if Connie ever did find someone to chair the committee, but I really didn't see a need for a whole committee to be set up just for...."

"Silence! I didn't ask your opinion! I don't want your opinion! This is a National Cancer Association event!" he shouted back at her. His lips were taut and his eyes narrowed again as he glared at her.

Alison smiled and replied, "Please calm down. Your attitude won't help. Now, what's the problem?" Alison studied the short stocky man, distracted by every detail of his appearance. Were those blonde hairs plugged onto his head, she wondered. Yes, they were! And he plucks his eyebrows! The short man's face was turning red. She could see that his face had now taken on the look of a predator stalking his prey. "What an unpleasant, ugly little person," Alison thought to herself. "What's really going on here?"

"What is motivating this public intimidation tactic? Alison wondered. She knew that confronting this type of agressive behavior with equal hostility wouldn't solve anything, and it may be seen as a ploy to provoke him further. So, with that reasoning in mind, she simply smiled back at the little man in front of her and calmly said, "Now, how can I help you?"

"What did you do with the money?" he asked.

"What money are you talking about? You really aren't making any sense."

"You know very well what money. The money you collected for the ribbon-running table," he said in sheer annoyance, his eyes narrowing.

"I put it in the cash box, of course," Alison said innocently. That seemed obvious. But she felt there was something sinister she had missed. "What's he up to?" she wondered.

The man then looked around at the crowd standing behind

him. He waited until he knew all eyes were on him. Mitch was there, silently clapping his hands together and bobbing his head up and down, encouraging the little man. Mr. Wall Street was standing next to Mitch with his arms folded across his chest and a big smirking grin on his face. Juanita Montoya seemed in a foul mood, as though her tight black pants were riding up on her—which seemed fitting.

The music from the field had stopped now. A few walkers still remained on the track, but most had gathered at one end, where whispered conversation could be heard.

Then the short stocky man asked, "What did you do with the cash box? Answer me! What did you do with the cash box?"

The crowd was silent with anticipation.

"I took it...," Alison began.

"Ah ha!" the man roared hysterically, his arms in the air, waving over his head. The sound pounced on Alison's words, cutting her off in mid-sentence. She now realized she was being played. "This fellow should be medicated," she thought. This whole thing was absurd.

"Just as I thought, she admitted it! She took it!" the small man shouted.

At that moment, Juanita Montoya stepped from the crowd and screamed, "Thief, I'll have your head!"

"This is a ridiculous accusation!" Alison countered, laughing at the lunacy.

"Silence! You stole *my* money!" Juanita Montoya shouted back at her. Alison knew she must somehow show how crazy these NCA people were.

"I will *not* be silent! No one has stolen any money! If you will let me finish...." Alison tried impatiently to get the words out but was shouted down each time by the short stocky man. She was losing her temper. It was late, already well past midnight. She was tired, hungry, and in need of sleep.

"I will have your head!" Juanita screamed at Alison... Then she got very quiet, moving closer into Alison's face; her words now could only be heard by the two of them. In a deep, low voice, she hissed, "How dare you, you belligerent peasant. We *are* the National Cancer Association...we will begin processing papers on you in the morning."

Alison was amused and started laughing again at the woman. "Did you all hear that?" she continued to laugh. "She said she was going to process papers on me.... What does that mean? Do I look like a desk...? ... process papers. For what? You don't have any proof that a crime was committed." Alison continued to laugh, and some in the crowd joined in. She knew Juanita's remarks were hollow threats to only intimidate and bully her. The tactic was very often successful in a court of law, but this woman was an amateur.

"Do you have any idea how ridiculously you are behaving?" Alison scolded. "You truly are an embarrassment to the National Cancer Association." she was speaking loudly enough for the crowd to hear. "Such childish behavior...and in the presence of these wonderful volunteers... You should be ashamed of yourself, Ms. Montoya."

The woman stared at Alison in disbelief, her beady black eyes narrowing. Then, turning to face the crowd, she slowly smoothed her black tunic by running her hands down the front of her body. The people began to part in front of her like the Red Sea as she walked through the gathered crowd to the parking lot; some hooting and slight applause could be heard. The short stocky man seemed to have lost touch with reality; still acting on his false perception, he faced the crowd and—in a prevailing tone—loudly announced, "You all heard her! She admitted it herself...that she took it! There is no denying it! She said herself; she took it!" He was shouting hysterically and didn't seem in control. "We all heard it...we all heard it. She said she took it! The National Cancer Association will handle this theft. We know how to deal with dishonesty and deceit. And let this be a lesson to anyone else who thinks about stealing from the National Cancer Association."

Then he turned in the direction of the woman in black who had just parted the crowd and trotted quickly, two-stepping to catch up with her. Then Mitch turned to the Mr. Wall Street, giving him a high five. Both walked away following the other two. Marcia and Alan Gross trailed behind. Alison stood there, stunned. The absurdity of what had just happened was whirling in her tired mind.

The procession disappeared into the darkness of the parking lot. The sound of car engines starting could be heard. They were leaving. Then Connie came up to Alison, "See, I told you, Alison… You asked too many questions, and they didn't like your attitude… Ya know, you should've been more agreeable…more vague…more submissive."

"Or perhaps more aggressive, more bullying, more intimidating—more like them?" The question hung in the air for a long moment as the two tired women stared at each other.

Then Connie quietly replied, "I was really very proud of you, Alison. You stood your ground and made them look like the fools they are."

"Okay, you and I know that…so why do you all put up with them? Don't you know they need *you*…not the other way around?! As a friend, we seriously need to talk about this," Alison said. "It's not a healthy situation."

Alison was familiar with this kind of bullying and intimidation. It was like emotional arsenic. If given in small doses over time, it slowly wears you down until you're afraid to think on your own. You become dependent… It's like being intellectually paralyzed; you lose confidence in your own judgment and can't function out of fear of criticism or abuse. A person in this state becomes a servant to whoever is inflicting the criticism and pressure. Alison had seen this happen in a corporate setting and knew that it had broken many a good manager. The usual reason that intimidation and bullying were inflicted was the need or obsession for control. And it was common knowledge that any obsessive need to control comes from an insecurity or some other egocentric neurosis. "This profile certainly fits the staff of the NCA—especially Juanita Montoya," Alison thought.

"Yes, I know you're right. It's been getting worse every year. All they want is more money from us." Connie confessed.

"Oh, speaking of money—I gave the cash box to Libby, like you told me to do. I did take it…but I took it *over* to Libby when I started walking the track. That's what they didn't want to hear. They wanted me to cower in front of them and to question myself," Alison said.

"Oh, I know—and yes, we do need to talk. But I'm not worried about the cash box. If I see Libby, I'll ask her about it. It will turn up. Now, why don't you go back home and see if you can get a few hours of sleep? I'm going home to do that myself…and at my age, I need my beauty rest!" Connie added, trying to make light of what had just happened. "Why don't we meet back here at 6 in the morning for coffee and a donut?" Connie said. "And don't worry about anything," she added reassuringly.

"That sounds like a great idea," Alison said. "See you in the morning…." Then, realizing the hour, she added with a chuckle, "…In a new light." Connie understood her meaning.

"Thanks Connie," Alison said as both women hugged each other and left for their cars.

❦ Chapter Twenty ❧

The next morning, Alison woke at 5:30. She had had a restless sleep, hoping that the events of the night before were just a bad dream.

She couldn't shake the nightmare images of Mitch or Juanita from her mind. But not all of it was unpleasant, she remembered. Her walk with Ruth and Janet had been very honest and personally enlightening—not just about Janet and Ruth, but about Connie. Their high praise of her gave Alison reassurance that Connie would understand and do the right thing when she learned more about the National Cancer Association.

Seeing the time on the digital clock that sat on the table next to the bed, Alison hurried downstairs to let out Dinah, who was already waiting at her doggie door. Alison gave the Dobie a dog cookie and opened the back door. After she trotted outside, Alison closed the door and unlatched the doggie door so Dinah could come back in to eat her morning kibbles. Then Alison rushed upstairs for a quick shower. After dressing in clean jeans and a t-shirt, she said good-bye to Dinah. Knowing she would not be gone all day, she let the dog have the run of the backyard.

On the drive over to the high school, Alison rolled all the windows down, hoping it would clear the ugly images of Mitch and Juanita from her mind. It was a beautiful clear morning; the cool, crisp air washed into the Jeep, swirling with new promise of optimism and adventure. This was Alison's favorite part of the day, when she usually walked Dinah and did her thinking. Now Dinah wasn't with her, but she sure had to do some thinking.

Once at the high school, she parked close to the entrance gate, knowing her Jeep would be used to haul the tables and chairs back to Connie's garage. Some of the participants were also bringing their cars around, anticipating the end of the event. Alison knew there were announcements and awards to be made, and all that would take place before the official ending at ten that morning. She entered the field and saw a few people still walking around the dirt track. The smell of coffee and bacon was wafting on the morning air. "Tent City" was coming to life. On the other side of the field, inside the breakfast tent, Alison found Connie sitting with Libby, the finance committee's chairperson.

"Hey, there—sit down and join us for some coffee," Connie said, greeting Alison.

"Thanks, that sounds great," she said. "Hi, Libby."

"Good morning." Libby got up and poured a cup of coffee, then came back to the table and set it down in front of Alison.

"Thanks," Alison said with a tired smile.

"We don't have time this morning to go into detail, Alison, so you'll have to save your hair-splitting questions for later," Connie said with a patient smile. "What's important for you to know is that Libby called me late last night—or, actually, early this morning—she had the cash box for the ribbon runners."

"I knew it!" Alison said. "Those staffers from NCA *wanted* people to think I stole the cash box."

"Well, either that, or they were just overly paranoid about the money," Libby offered.

"Thanks Libby, but that really doesn't help," Connie said, a bit annoyed.

"Sorry…anyway, I have to find Marge—she said she would go with me to make the final deposit." Libby got up from the table and went off looking for Marge.

The two women sat quietly, then Connie spoke. "Alison, you deserve an explanation for everything, and you'll get one, but now is not the time. Right now, I just need your help in breaking down the event and cleaning up…will you still help me?"

"Sure," Alison said. "Oh, will there be any NCA staff here today?"

"Usually not," Connie said. "They rarely show up for the closing ceremony, but because of what happened last night—and because there are six of them—they may decide to show up again.

"But if you're anxious to say good-bye, you might find them all at the Saturday brunch buffet at the four-star hotel down the road," Connie added with a sarcastic grin.

"No, thank you!" Alison said emphatically. "I just wanted to know if I'll be able to keep my breakfast down." Both women began to laugh as they got up from the bench. "It's going to be a good day," Alison thought to herself.

๛ Chapter Twenty-one ๛

Without the hovering appearance of the staff from the National Cancer Association, the morning went smoothly. Inside the breakfast tent, the participants all enjoyed coffee and donuts provided by the local women's club. The sounds of kids playing kickball came from somewhere on the field as squad participants began arranging chairs in front of the stage, anticipating the announcements starting at nine. There would be awards for the most miles marched and the best homemade apple pie, as well as the best costume participants. Most people enjoyed the closing ceremony, gathering to say good-bye to friends and neighbors and to hear the final tallies on funds raised.

It was a little before 9:30 and Connie was on stage now, checking out the sound system. From her vantage point, she was the first to spot them getting out of the large gold Cadillac Escalade: They were all coming to the award ceremony. Juanita Montoya was leading the group across the track toward the stage, dodging people whose arms were loaded with boxes and ice coolers. Connie caught Alison's attention, gave her a look, and nodded her head a few times in their direction. Alison, who was standing off by the breakfast tent, looked where Connie was nodding and saw the reason for her changed expression.

"Oh dear—it *was* a nice day…" she thought as she returned a look of foreboding.

Connie quickly spoke into the microphone, "Please, good people of Rosemont…Rosemont!" The sound reverberated from the field's public address system that had just been turned on. "Please gather round. We have some announcements and some surprises for you.

"QUIET, PLEASE!" Connie waited until the voices from the crowd lowered to a murmur. "Thank you all for your participation in this year's annual event. We all know why we come each year. For most of us, it's because we have lost someone to cancer. That's what we all have in common. Let us always remember them…and thank you again for coming and sharing."

There was sincere applause from the gathered crowd and Connie graciously thanked them with a modest nod and smile. Then she continued, "I would first like to thank the committee chairs…," and, as Connie named off each chairperson, they stood up in the crowd and accepted the warm recognition and applause from their friends. There were some hoots and hollers, all meant in familiar teasing. When the noise died down, a special thanks went out to the BBQ attendants and the others who worked behind the scenes.

Then Connie's voice came through the PA system, "Now, for the squad totals.…" She announced the dollars that each of the ten squads had raised and turned in to Libby for the event. After each squad was announced, they all got up together and accepted the cheers and applause. During the announcement of squad totals, Alison had brought one of the folding chairs from the breakfast tent over for herself. She now was viewing the stage from the front row—stage left.

"And now, the total from this year's ribbon-runners donations!" Connie's voice had changed to a strong deliberate tone as she looked over at Juanita Montoya and the National Cancer Association gang; all were now standing together to the right of the stage. They returned only dumb stares.

"With the help of my dear friend, Alison...," Connie paused and gazed in Alison's direction, "...we received a total of $523.50 in donations. That's a new best for Rosemont!" Connie exclaimed with pride. The crowd applauded and now noticed where Alison was sitting.

"And now I would like to introduce someone whom I'm sure you all know, Ms. Juanita Montoya, Executive Vice President of the Colorado Division of the National Cancer Association. She will be announcing this year's overall event total."

There was the same polite applause Alison had heard at the Recruitment Rally coming from those gathered. Connie held out the microphone with a clipboard to Juanita as she stepped up onstage. As she walked over toward Connie, she began to slowly run her hands down the front of the same black outfit, her red beaded necklace swinging from side to side across her small bosom. With no acknowledgement or thank-you to Connie, the woman grabbed the microphone and clipboard, then began to address the crowd.

"Thank you...thank you all for that warm reception."

"What warm reception?" Alison thought to herself. Connie caught Alison's eye and smiled.

The woman was now looking down at the clipboard in her hand and seemed more irritated than usual. Then she spoke.

"The National Cancer Association would like to take this opportunity to thank the community of Rosemont for all the hard work they have done for our organization. We at the National Cancer Association are pleased we could bring this national event to your community. The money you raised during this event will provide the National Cancer Association the means to follow our mission—a cure for cancer. And now, this year's total...." As she continued, the entire crowd got on their feet and applauded

Alison turned to watch folks shaking each other's hands, patting each other on the back, and some of the women standing were hugging each other.

"This is what it should be about—a community effort," Alison thought. "Maybe this is why Connie is involved. Juanita Montoya probably thinks they are applauding her," she chuckled to herself.

While people were still standing and cheering, Juanita loudly spoke in a haughty tone, "Please, please—*I am not finished.*" The crowd quieted a bit. "You all know—as *we* do—that this total did not reach the dollar goal set for your community by the National Cancer Association. What this means is that next year, you must try much harder. Next year, your dollar goal will be even higher. With the help of the National Cancer Association, we expect you to reach that dollar goal!"

Alison could feel the kick in her stomach and the wind taken out of these people's sails. Before they barely had a moment to revel in their achievement, this woman was belittling them, telling them that what they did, all the sacrifices they made, all the time they gave—the committee meetings, the car washes, the cake sales—wasn't good enough. Alison could feel their disappointment, and she watched as their enthusiasm dissolved. The crowd was still.

"Well, again—thank you all from the National Cancer Association...and good luck next year!" The woman smugly said with a sneer. There was no more applause from the crowd. She began walking over to Connie, who was standing to the left of the stage. With a smirking grin, she handed the microphone and clipboard back to her. Not a word was shared between the two women. She turned her back to Connie and started walking back across the stage, back to her waiting entourage. The sound of her long, striding steps pounding the flimsy wooden stage floor was all that was heard.

Connie, now with the microphone in hand, broke the silence and loudly said, "Aren't you forgetting something, Ms. Montoya?"

The crowd was silent. The woman stopped and turned.

"Nooo…I don't think so…." she said, displaying a sense of contrived innocence. The crowd was now so silent that there was no need for the microphone Connie was using. The two women standing alone on the stage could be easily heard.

"I think you have," Connie continued. The crowd sensed the tension between them and was riveted. More people were gathering now, just like last night when Alison was accused of stealing. "I think you need to apologize," Connie said loudly, and she seemed to intentionally draw out the exchange so more of the folks on the field could listen.

"I don't know what you are talking about," Juanita countered nervously. The two were now facing each other on the stage in front of the entire community of Rosemont.

"Last night, without knowing the truth, you—representing the National Cancer Association—accused my dear friend, Alison, of stealing 'your' money," Connie said loudly into the microphone as she pointed in Alison's direction. Alison picked up a slight quiver in Connie's voice.

"Oh, that…nothing more than a silly mistake. No need to get all worked up, dearie," the woman said flippantly as she waved her hand at Connie, brushing away the remark. She avoided any look in Alison's direction.

"That was a serious accusation about the character of my friend, and this community expects *you* to apologize to her—on behalf of the National Cancer Association, of course," Connie said, holding her ground.

Deception in a Small Town

"There is no need to apologize. My statements last night were based on the information at the time. And so you see, there's no need for an apology." Her eyes squinting, the woman's thin lips pursed as she glared back at Connie. Once again, Juanita's face got as red as the beads around her neck. Connie held the microphone out between them as the woman came closer, saying in a low voice, "*Do not* challenge me—I *am* the National Cancer Association."

Juanita heard her own sinister voice echo across the field. No other sound was heard. Then she turned her back on Connie and walked off the stage. Connie looked over at Alison and gave her a smile. Alison mouthed the words, "Thank you," to Connie.

Connie waited until Juanita and her entourage were well off the field. Then a single slow clapping could be heard from somewhere in the crowd. Others joined the clapping until everyone was applauding the woman standing alone on the little stage.

"Thank you all again," Connie said. "I officially declare this event closed."

She put the microphone down and stepped off the stage. Walking over to Alison, she smiled with relief, saying, "That's done! Now let's put this puppy to bed."

Alison just remained standing there at the end of the stage. "That was amazing. Connie, thank you for standing up for me," Alison said, giving her a big hug.

"Hey, I always stand up for my friends. Like I said, we'll have time to talk about it later."

As Alison worked, folding and stacking the chairs in sets of five next to the tables by the entrance gate, she realized the significance of what had just happened. If Connie had not confronted this woman, Alison could have been labeled dishonest or, even worse, a thief. She had learned that, in a small town, a person's integrity is greatly valued. It can determine your influence in the community, even more so than your wealth. She had learned that from Connie, too. Connie could have easily sided with the National Cancer Association and held Alison in contempt until the cash box was found; even worse, she could have hidden or tampered with the box when Libby wasn't looking, to support the organization's position. But Alison shook that thought, knowing how out of character it would be for Connie. When Connie asked for an apology, it was in defense of Alison's good name and the truth; it showed this community that Alison was one who could be trusted. She then realized why the women of this small community had such love and respect for Connie. It was all very real now and made sense.

Alison continued to stack everything near the field gates. The banners were rolled and banded; the trash bags tied up and piled near the dumpster. After helping with the setup, Alison was familiar with the break down. They loaded Connie's car first, then Alison's. Connie stayed behind with Bert to answer any final questions and make sure the athletic field gates were securely locked.

Alison got in her car and started back to Connie's, unloading once she arrived. She was so tired, but she knew if she kept moving, she would stay awake. She wanted to wait for instructions from Connie on arranging the items inside, so she stacked things alongside the garage. There would be a trip to the National Cancer Association in Fremont in the next few weeks, and Alison wasn't sure what would stay with Connie and what would go back to the Fremont office.

Once finished, she drove home, leaving the driveway open for Connie's SUV. Alison said hello to Dinah, then walked back out and around the corner to Connie's. It was almost noon when Connie drove into the driveway. Alison hadn't been waiting long.

"Good job!" Connie said as she got out of her SUV. The two continued to work in numb exhaustion, unloading Connie's the SUV and arranging and organizing everything in the garage so it all fit.

"There's one last trip to Fremont with all the NCA banners and boxes, but that's not until after the R & R meeting in two weeks," Connie said.

"Rest and relaxation?" Alison said jokingly. "I could sure use that!" She recalled that the fundraising process had started in early spring, before she had even arrived in Rosemont; it was now late summer, and there were still more meetings. "Does this ever stop?" Alison wondered.

"No, it stands for Recap and Review. That's when the committee chairs all get together and turn in unused supplies and tell each other how the logistics and procedures can be improved for next year," Connie said. "But I like to think of it as really just an excuse for pizza and beer."

"Well deserved, I'm sure." Alison said.

"I was hoping the trip to Fremont would be after the Reno Rendezvous," Connie said as she closed and locked her car doors.

"Reno Rendezvous?" Alison hesitated, almost afraid to ask.

Taking a big breath, Connie leaned up against the car and explained. "Reno Rendezvous is just a big expensive three-day party the National Cancer Association throws every year. There are thousands of attendees from all over the Western United States.

"I went two years ago," she said. "The attendees include head volunteers and staff members from all the different community marches from each of the towns and cities that hosts a March at Night Event…and that's why I don't want to go to Fremont before the Reno Rendezvous, because they'll ask me to go again this year and, personally, I think it's an expensive waste of time. Oh, it was great to get out and see a big city like Reno, but they kept such a tight leash on us that we didn't get out at all, and many of the expenses aren't covered. It cost me money I really couldn't afford.

"It seemed to me that it was more of an opportunity for the executives and staff members of the organization to give themselves a big pat on the back. The NCA must spend hundreds of thousands of dollars over those three days. They pay for everyone's travel, room, and meals. Hundreds of people come—they rent a huge hotel convention hall and fly in these guest speakers. It's a great audiovisual presentation, but still just a lot of symbolism," Connie said. "It's like a really big recruitment party."

It sounded to Alison like a new drug launch event. She had attended many of these events in resort areas while working for Merck Pharmaceuticals. It was one thing for a profitable corporation to spend money thanking investors and stockholders, as well as inspiring a sales force with the approval of a new product, but quite another for a nonprofit organization to spend donor dollars on huge expensive travel trips and call them "teaching programs." How did this meet their mission statement? At the moment, though, Alison didn't have the energy to get angry.

"Anyway, how did I get on that tired subject?" Connie reflected.

Finding this a good time to change the subject, Alison asked, "Why don't you come over for dinner tomorrow night, Connie? I still need to know the details of the missing cash box, and I don't want to leave Dinah home alone another night. I have some fresh zucchini from the garden," Alison bribed.

"Only if I can bring over some yellow squash," Connie countered.

Both women started laughing, knowing that everyone had a bumper crop this year.

"See ya around 6 o'clock? We'll eat on the patio."

"Sounds great!"

❧ Chapter Twenty-two ❧

The next evening, Alison was preparing for her company. She was going to serve a zucchini quiche and a garden green salad with bread she had bought fresh that morning. A peach cobbler was planned for dessert. Alison really enjoyed the fresh produce that was available during the summer months in this rural farming community. Connie had called that morning and offered to contribute a bottle of white wine produced locally, and Alison was delighted.

It was just before six; Alison had fed Dinah and was setting the table outside on the back porch when Connie came to the backyard gate. Dinah knew Connie well and, with a friendly bark, let Alison know that company had arrived.

Alison came to the back gate. "Hi. Come on in…I just have to toss the salad, then we can eat." The evenings were getting shorter now, and sometimes the clouds would build for a late evening thundershower. As Alison went into the kitchen, she noticed the clouds building to the southwest. "I hope we can at least get through the meal before the rain comes," she said.

"Yup," Connie said, then added, "can I help?"

"Sure, come on in. You can open the wine."

With the bottle now opened, Connie asked, "Where are the glasses?"

"Outside on the table," was the reply. Once the wine was poured, the two women held up their glasses. Connie offered the toast as they clinked them together. "To good friends and good health!"

"Here, here!" Alison seconded.

They began exchanging compliments and recipes over their meal. Alison was pleased with how it had turned out; she was still a bit unsure of cooking at this altitude.

After dinner was over, the two women remained on the porch, enjoying the cool evening air. As Alison filled Connie's wine glass, she asked, "So tell me—what happened after we both left on Friday night?"

"Well, I was just getting into bed when Libby called. Some of her committee members couldn't stay to help count the money from the event, so I told her to lock it all up and I'd be in early on Saturday to help with the final tally. We had it under control.

"You see, Alison, Libby had made the scheduled night drop at 10:30 Friday night then she went home…that's where she called me from …her home. She didn't mention that the ribbon-runner money was in that night bank drop, because the Friday night deposit always included the cash from the ribbon runners." Connie explained. "She wasn't there on the field when they accused you of stealing, so she won't think to mention it. So of course, that's when I asked her if she had the cash box and the ribbon-runner money, and that's when she told me she had deposited it on Friday night with the rest of the funds. When we met for coffee Saturday morning I told her what happened and asked her to let me apologize to you. I felt really bad, but we still had to the event to close and no time for a length discussion."

"So that's when you learned that Libby had the cash box for the ribbon runners?"

"Friday night, I told you everything would be okay. Didn't I?" Connie said. Alison looked a bit annoyed.

"I knew I was going to see you in a few hours, and I was so tired…and knowing all the questions you can come up with, I didn't want to have to start explaining all the details over the phone. If I had called you then, at one o'clock in the morning, I knew I wouldn't get any sleep that night," Connie said with a smile. She'd just proved her point. Alison now understood the reasoning.

"So, it's my fault," Alison said reflectively. "Isn't that ironic. Usually questions are asked to uncover the truth, not an excuse for withholding the truth."

"Well, I'm sorry. Please forgive my timing on this…there were no malicious intentions, and we told you the first thing in the morning. Libby felt kinda bad, but she knew that you and I were friends and that I knew best."

"Yes, we *are* friends, aren't we?" Alison said. She thought that maybe this was the time to tell Connie what she had learned about the organizations Connie volunteered for…but first, Alison was curious. "Connie, why do you continue as a volunteer for these people, when there is so much to be done right here on the home front—I mean, locally?"

"There you go with the questions again. I've been asking myself the same thing…but now that someone else is asking, I suppose I really should face the question. Ya know how easy it is to avoid a question when you're only asking yourself?" Connie said evasively, again looking to Alison for understanding. Alison thought about her move to the Colorado and how hard that had been to face.

"What really makes me mad," Alison began. "Is that the National Cancer Association has turned a scientific issue into an emotional one. Most people don't understand what cancer is—how many forms it takes, how long it has plagued life on earth."

"What do you mean?"

"If people understood what cancer is, they would see that it occurs in all life-forms—from a tree in the forest to frogs in a pond—and that it's been around for thousands of years."

"I had no idea," Connie said.

"People don't realize that it has been around as long as life has been on earth. The disease has been given many other names, because it comes in so many different forms, but it's still the same basic mechanism. It's merely an error in the genetic material of a cell. Theoretically, if a living being has DNA, that living being has the potential to develop cancer."

"Go on," Connie said.

"You see...when a cell in your body—or in any living organism— for that matter, divides, which they do millions of times during their lifetimes, the newly divided cell may have a mistake in its genetic material, or DNA. The more cells in a body, the more chances of a mistake—that's just a statistical law of probability."

"That's frightening," Connie said. "I only taught eighth grade biology, but it sounds like more people should be dying of cancer. What's preventing that from happening?" she asked.

"Our immune systems...," Alison said matter-of-factly, "...the same system that cures the common cold and heals a scratch on your leg. One of the more important functions of the immune system is to kills the abnormal cells or the new cell with mistaken DNA before that cell can divide and become a cancer. Cancer is simply a normal cell gone wrong.

"The other reason that more deaths are not caused by cancer is...well...I had a very brilliant professor when I was in graduate school—he was somewhat of a cynic, but a great scientist; in many ways, his studies advanced the scientific understanding of tumor growth."

"Is he still alive?" Connie asked.

"No…and that's my point—he didn't die of cancer, he died of a heart attack when he was only 54 years old. Statistically, he should have gotten some sort of cancer later on in life, but he never made it to old age.

"There are so many other causes of death, man-made and otherwise—like wars, car accidents, plane crashes, or those that are self-inflicted like alcoholism, drug abuse, or suicide. Think of all the people who have died prematurely from natural disasters like tornados, floods, and earthquakes. All these causes of death are what control the world's population. So, for those who are not affected by these population controls—the people who grow older—their chances of getting cancer increase."

"How depressing, Alison. I don't know if I want to hear more," Connie said.

"But here's the good news—if there is any— is the interesting fact that each cancer is unique."

"Really? I know that both Frank and my John died of prostate cancer. Prostate cancer is prostate cancer…isn't it?" Connie asked.

"Well, yes and no," Alison said.

"Well now, that sounds real scientific," Connie replied, frustrated with such a vague answer.

"'Yes' because the tissue from both men's prostates functions similarly, but 'no' because each man is a unique individual, and that makes his cancer as unique as he is. I'm sure you've heard stories of people who respond differently to the same cancer treatment? Well, that's one of the reasons why. In the research laboratory at the Huntsman Cancer Institute in Salt Lake City—it's a private hospital, not government supported—the doctors and scientists test each individual's cancer and tailor a treatment specifically for that person's cancer cells. They do wonderful work and get very good results. They really take into consideration the uniqueness of each individual. Let's see…an example would be—if two women were both diagnosed with breast cancer; both cancers, at the same stage of development, are tested for the hormone response of the tumor—one responds, the other doesn't. So those two women will have different treatments. While most large hospitals have a tumor board that goes over each cancer case, most treatment centers don't have the resources for individualized medications, so everyone gets the same one. And the result is that not everyone is cured by the same treatment."

"I never realized...," Connie said reflectively.

"It's also just a game of chance; some people have better odds than others," Alison continued.

"That can't be good.... What do you mean?" Connie asked.

"Well, a lot of people inherit bad cells from one of their parents, and when it's that cell's turn to divide, the error is expressed, and a cancer forms. Many people increase their chances of getting cancer by smoking or getting too much sun, and we've known for years about cancer-causing agents, called 'carcinogens.' But this doesn't mean everyone who smokes or gets sunburned will get cancer; it just increases the chances.

"So you see, cancer isn't going away. There isn't a magic bullet that will cure it which isn't to say there aren't some genetic research labs working on one. There are just some common sense ways to reduce your chances of getting cancer—like keeping your immune system healthy by eating fruits and vegetables—but most people don't need a government agency spending hundreds of thousands of dollars to tell them that. People still make their own choices.

"So if we accept the premise that cancer can't be totally prevented, then the next step is early diagnosis; the earlier any cancer is detected, the better the chances are that a treatment will work." Alison looked away from Connie, seemingly distracted and then added, "Boy—I have to tell you, I got so upset the other night when I was watching the news. The announcer said that pap smears prevent vaginal cancer in women. That information is false and such a disservice to the public! Pap smears cannot *prevent* cancer; they can only *detect* it. If a cancer is found, it still has to be treated. There's a vaccine now that will boost the immune system to recognize certain forms of virally caused vaginal cancers and stop their growth. This knucklehead announcer suggested that a pap test would take the place of the vaccine. Then he talked about insurance coverage. Actually, young women can get the vaccine free from the pharmaceutical company if their families financially qualify."

"Really?" Connie said.

"Yes! And I felt like getting on the web and telling the news station to clear their health information with a professional, because this fellow sure lacked correct medical information. But, I digress."

"Here, have another glass of wine," Connie offered.

"Thanks," Alison said. "I think I shall."

As Connie poured the wine, Alison thought that if she was making the foundation of her argument too complex or entangled, Connie would lose interest. She knew that if she couldn't keep Connie engaged in an intellectual view of the discussion, then she might fall back into the emotional attitude that most people seemed to share about a cure for cancer.

"There…now go on, please," Connie encouraged, much to Alison's relief.

"Thanks. Well, then the last area is treatment, which is always changing…not so much the drugs that are used against the cancer—there haven't been many new drugs approved recently by the FDA. As you may know, an approval is needed before it is allowed on the market."

"Of course, but why so few new drugs?"

"It takes years for a pharmaceutical company to get new drug approvals, and millions of dollars in preclinical testing as well as the expensive clinical drug trials that could take years and require a certain number of patients in order to be considered statistically significant. Even after a drug is approved the Pharmaceutical companies are federally required to do follow-up safety studies on the new drug."

"I had no idea," Connie said.

"That's why oftentimes, doctors work on new *ways* to deliver the currently approved drugs. There are some exciting breakthroughs in this area that reduce the general side effects patients suffer from the drugs. More often, doctors will combine the drugs into what's called a 'drug cocktail.' The combination of drugs is determined based on the side effects of each one; the idea is not to compound the side effects. Understand?" Alison paused, realizing that Connie's eyes seemed glazed over, either from the wine or the information.

"Connie, you really didn't want to know all this, did you?" Alison asked.

"Well, in all fairness, I didn't expect it. But, really, I have found it interesting. There was so much I didn't understand during John's treatment."

"I'm sorry—my intention was only to point out that cancer has been around a long time and there isn't a simple cure. What the National Cancer Association is selling isn't scientific...it's emotional," Alison said, then waited until that sunk in. There was silence between the two women.

"Sooo...what you're saying is that most of the donations people give, thinking they are helping find a cure for cancer, are really only helping the organization's effort to keep the focus on emotional symbolism."

"Exactly,' Alison said, glad her efforts weren't in vain. "Think about it, Connie: What if a cure for cancer was discovered? It would put them out of business. Do you really think they would support a discovery like that? Do you really think they would jeopardize business as usual? Understand one thing: A cure for cancer is bad for their business! The National Cancer Association *is* a business, and it involves millions and millions of dollars, corporate offices, advertising agencies, executives, employees, pension plans, Federal bureaucracies, and retirement funds. As a corporation classified as a 501-C3, their tax-exempt status only requires them to contribute a small portion of their donated income to research. Last year, they gave only 15% of all their donor dollars to research, and they spent 20% of those donor dollars on fundraising. Once a community like Rosemont turns over their donations to the National Cancer Association, that organization can direct your money in any area of science they choose—and do you really think that they would want to put it into a discovery that would put them out of business?" There was silence again.

"That's very cynical of you, Alison," Connie accused.

"Perhaps, but it *is* the unfortunate truth," Alison countered sympathetically. Connie seemed suspicious.

"What you're saying is that only 15 cents of every dollar we raised here in Rosemont went to cancer research?" Connie looked as if she had seen a ghost.

Then Alison went on, "Assuming that cancer will always be a medical challenge with no silver bullets, the questions become, How can we help those who are suffering from the disease? and How can we save more lives? These questions require practical answers—early diagnosis and treatment—not emotional ones…don't you agree?" Alison asked.

"So remember, I'm just a newcomer to Rosemont: Tell me how the National Cancer Association has helped the folks in rural Colorado with early diagnosis or treatments?"

"Not much...I see your point," Connie said. Then she countered, "Well, in all fairness, some of their programs that they have available really *do* help people who have cancer."

"And how many programs have you seen come to rural Colorado? Is that what all your hard work and sacrifice has been about for the past three years?" Alison replied.

"You're right about that," Connie reflected.

"I'm sure there are some well-meaning people working for the National Cancer Association who really do believe they are helping—people who have lost a loved one to cancer like you. Others just like the feeling of importance they get by working for a national organization; some just need a job. Their motives are not on trial.

"But if they knew the truth about the organization they worked or volunteered for, what would they do? That's why this is so important, Connie," Alison declared in a pleading tone. "People need to know the facts, and with that knowledge they can make up their own minds and choose to donate their hard-earned money or not. If they still want to donate, they should know how it's being spent. If they don't like how it's being spent, they should stop giving. The same is true if they choose to volunteer for a fundraiser: They should know who is benefiting from their time. Everyone should know the truth in order to choose wisely," Alison said. She hoped that Connie didn't see that last remark as derogatory. She certainly didn't mean to say that the folks who had just finished volunteering for the National Cancer Association fundraiser were simply ignorant and emotional. Just the opposite, in fact: In the short time Alison had lived in Rosemont, she had found its residents to be generous and genuine and to possess more common sense than half the state of New Jersey.

"What if all the months of time and effort the volunteers gave to this year's National Cancer Association March at Night went towards our own local nonprofits who help our local folks who have cancer? Just think about it...," Alison pleaded.

Connie seemed reflective, but finally she said, "You're right about that. Those women over at Bosom Buddies really helped when Janet got breast cancer three years ago. As Jimmy's teacher, I stayed close to the family."

"Yes, Janet told me," Alison said, watching Connie sip her wine, deep in thought. Then Alison said, "I did a little research on the nonprofits here in Rosemont County. There are quite a few, and some are very generous organizations—like the Caring Friends Fund: They give monetary support directly to patients stricken with cancer to pay for food, utilities, and medications. You can't keep the money more local than that!" Alison said, feeling better now that she had said how she felt about the generosity being provided locally.

"Ya know...you're right," Connie said slowly. "I remember...last year, after the community asked the National Cancer Association for a grant for our new Cancer Center, and they turned us down, the local car club had a fundraiser and donated $40,000 for the needed hospital equipment," she reflected.

"That's just wonderful," Alison replied. "I found the people I met over at the Cancer Center very nice as well," she added.

A dubious look came over Connie's face. Alison, feeling that the mood may have changed, suggested they go into the house for dessert.

"Let's have the peach cobbler and coffee in the living room...I can show you what I've done to the house," she offered pleasantly. They collected a few of the plates from the table and walked to the porch door. Once inside, Alison, taking the plates from Connie, said, "Oh, thanks—just make yourself at home." She turned on some lights down the hall and headed to the kitchen, followed by Dinah.

Connie wandered, looking at the art and browsing the titles on the spines of the books Alison had neatly organized on the built-in bookshelves at one end of the living room. Then Connie noticed that the doors were open to Alison's study across the hall. She had never been in this room. Alison had always had the doors closed on her past visits. Now she knew why: There was a desk with stacks of papers and books. A computer keyboard and mouse were perched on one of the stacks, and she noticed CDs and DVDs in organized piles on the floor.

Then she saw the bookshelves in the office, full of very thick, large tomes such as Goodman and Gilman's *The Pharmacological Basis of Therapeutics*. There was also a medical dictionary, a *Physician's Desk Reference*, and other medical reference books. As Connie surveyed the room, Alison hollered from the kitchen, "Decaf?"

"Yeah, that sounds great!" Connie hollered back. She was now surveying the walls that were covered with photos and awards. There was one from Habitat for Humanity of Newark, New Jersey. Connie recognized Alison in the picture, which had been taken some time ago. Alison, who looked very happy, was standing with a man, who Connie assumed was Jack. Another photo was of a group of men and women in white coats, posing in front of a large corporate-looking building. Connie found Alison in the front row, also wearing a white coat. There were a few plaques and awards hanging on the wall from different medical organizations, all with Alison's name on them. The one that caught Connie's eye was "Product Manager of the Year," from a company named Cyclacel. The date was only last year.

"So you found my hiding place?" Connie whirled around. Alison was now standing in the doorway, smiling and holding a tray full of dessert and coffee. Alison was amused by the surprised look on Connie's face. "I know you're wondering how someone who just moved in could have accumulated such an assortment of data storage paraphernalia...."

"Oh, I'm sorry.... The door was open...," Connie said a bit sheepishly. "You told me that you worked in an office back in New Jersey."

"Yes, there are lots of companies in New Jersey, and I *did* work in an office; what I *didn't* mention was that it was in a pharmaceutical company." Connie remained quiet and Alison continued. "After graduate school, I worked for many years for Merck Pharmaceuticals, and then, for the past five years, I worked for a small biotech company." Seeing the stunned look on Connie's face, Alison flippantly added, "…someone's gotta do it…," with a chuckle, trying to downplay the title and position. "Let's go into the living room," she said.

The two women, with Dinah trailing, went into the living room. It seemed to Alison that Connie had a million questions and just didn't know which to ask first.

"This is great peach cobbler," Connie said, breaking the silence.

"Well, they *were* locally grown peaches," Alison agreed, smiling. "That makes all the difference. Okay…what do you want to know?" she said to her friend.

"Why?" Connie said. "Why didn't you tell me your background was in cancer research and pharmaceuticals?"

"Two reasons, I guess. The first was just out of habit. I've learned over the years, especially while in college and graduate school, that when guys learned I was a science major, they expected me to be dull and boring. They were afraid they'd sound stupid, and then they didn't know what to talk about. Let me tell you, there were some real awkward moments. And the women often seemed unfriendly…I just didn't share their social interests. Even my own family had no idea what I was studying at the university, and no one ever asked. But science has always been my love and my life…that was before I met Jack, of course."

Not wanting to take the conversation down that path, Alison continued, "The second reason I didn't say anything about my past is because many people have misconceptions about drug companies in general. They think they are greedy, pill-pushing corporations that want to gouge the public. Many of these people may have had a bad experience with their medication, and people can't ignore their prejudices or their own experiences. But if people only knew how dedicated some of the scientists are who work in that industry..." Alison said, thinking of Jerry. "And besides, all those questions I asked of Mitch would have been suspect. You see? It's better that no one knew. Does that make sense?" Alison asked.

"Yes, I can see how your background would have influenced people's perceptions...and we sure do have our own opinions about things in this town," Connie emphasized.

"If I had told you everything I told you tonight, and if I had spoken out before the fundraiser, I can only imagine the rumors that would be flying around about the 'newcomer'—we probably wouldn't be friends now."

"You're right about that..." Connie agreed.

"At the time, I could see how involved you were with this year's community fundraiser...the *whole* community was involved...and because of what you told me about small towns and rumor mills, I realized the whole truth about my background and everything I said tonight would have only made things worse. And besides, if you had known about me then, what would you have done?" Alison questioned rhetorically.

"I don't know," Connie replied.

"I just couldn't put you in that position—the community was depending on you. So I waited," Alison said.

"So, you might say...it was like me waiting until the next morning to tell you about the cash box?" Connie said with a grin.

"Touché," Alison said, smiling. "Point well made. Do you see the dilemma you would have faced? On the one hand, you would know that the organization you were volunteering for was like a cheating spouse. Its representatives have been lying to you about their true motives. It's as if the NCA was having an affair with your donations, your money, and they used your emotions and losses to get at your money. That's how they lied to the community—they broke their promise to you: They broke that contract they signed. That contract was between the NCA and each member of the event committee. Again, I'm not suggesting the organization did anything illegal, but were they honest?"

Now Connie realized the reason for Alison's strange question about a cheating spouse...it all had to do with trust and ethics.

"I can't tell you how hard it was keeping my mouth shut, especially during the recruitment party. I just had to settle on simple questions to support the facts I was reading about in Professors Bennett and DiLorenzo's book, *Cancer Scam*...and I must say, the tactics used by the National Cancer Association are right out of the proverbial 'playbook' of the Advocacy Foundation mentioned in that book."

"Well, that explains all your questions...but *what* book?" Connie asked. Alison got up and went into her office; she came out with a narrow 200-page book. She handed it to Connie.

"I marked the pages that specifically apply to Colorado. It could explain why Rosemont never got that mobile X-ray machine you wanted," Alison said as Connie flipped to the page on the Brooks Trust. As she read, her eyes became large...then she put the book down.

"Oh, my God! Is this *true*?" She was in disbelief.

"Yes, I'm afraid so," Alison said. "Professor Bennett is a professor of economics at George Mason University. His reputation is stellar; his references and sources are excellent."

"Why haven't I heard about this before?" Connie said, bewildered.

Deception in a Small Town

"That, I can't answer. The Brooks Trust made the news before your involvement with the organization, but people have busy lives. You were probably teaching school and caring for your family. Most people wouldn't pay much attention to an obscure court hearing that happened during the holidays, most likely during a December snowstorm…and 15 years ago."

"Boy, have *we* been getting the snow job!" Connie said angrily.

"Well, if you had quit before the event, this community would have been disillusioned and bitter and blamed you—or more likely me! One of us would have been a scapegoat for all their disappointment. That wouldn't have been productive.

"So, now that you know, what'd you think should be done?" Alison asked. "This is a great community, full of people with generous hearts. I saw such warm, sharing feelings and honest emotions on the field the other night—it would be cruel to take that away and give them nothing to replace it with."

Connie spoke reluctantly. "I have to tell them, and I have to tell them why I can't do this any more. I have to share what I've learned with the whole community. They deserve to know.

"I know…I know. Some of the folks will be mad and direct their anger at me. I know that some others like the affiliation with a big national organization…it makes them feel important. Those folks will be mad and bitter regardless of the truth—they wouldn't choose to accept it anyway—and they'll call me a liar. I can live with that. But the majority will want…and deserve…to know the truth," Connie said, as if only to herself.

"I suppose the best time to tell them I'm quitting and why is at the R & R meeting; all the committee members will be there, and most of the squad leaders, too. I really wish I could tell Sally and Marge before the meeting—they're the hardest workers we have—but the way they gossip, we really wouldn't need to have a meeting, now would we?" Connie laughed. "Besides, I don't want my reasons filtered through anyone else.

I'll have to apologize to them individually after I make my announcement."

"Understand, Connie, that there will still be some people who'll think I put you up to this…that I changed your mind. You must tell them this was *your* own decision and give them *your* reasons," Alison insisted.

"Here, take the book with you, as you can see I have quite enough books to keep me busy," Alison said, smiling.

"Thanks, Alison, I will—and thanks for caring about me and our small community," Connie said sincerely.

"I want to call it *my* community, too," Alison said. The two women shared a hug.

"Would you like Dinah and me to walk you home?" Alison offered.

"No, thanks anyway," Connie replied. "I need some time alone to think."

"No problem. Have a good evening, dear friend," Alison said as she opened the front door. The nights were getting chilly, and she handed Connie a sweater hanging on the hook by the door. Connie threw it over her shoulders and walked down the steps to the sidewalk. Alison watched her disappear around the corner under the yellow glow of the old street lamp. She was relieved that the evening had gone so well.

ॐ Chapter Twenty-three ॐ

The next week went by fast for Alison. Her email box was full of unanswered mail that she needed to catch up on, and the house had been neglected to the point of disarray—not at all Alison's organized style. The days were getting shorter, so her walks with Dinah started later in the mornings. The district schools were now back in session. She saw the traditional yellow school bus on the main streets in town. Alison stayed busy at the library and farmers market, and chose not to call her friend, knowing Connie was a substitute teacher and this was a busy time for her. The space created between the two friends by other community obligations was welcomed by Alison.

Jimmy, who was back in school, now came over on Saturdays to mow the lawn. The big elm tree in the backyard was starting to shed leaves, and Alison reminded herself to ask him to rake before he mowed next week. Even the squirrel in the backyard, whom Alison had named Chuck—and who had tormented Dinah all summer long—was busy collecting his cache for the winter months. Fall was in the air.

Early Sunday evening, Alison realized the R & R meeting was in two days. Hoping she was still invited, she decided to call Connie and make sure.

"Hey, how's it going?" Alison asked in reply to the "Hello?" she heard when her call was answered.

"Fine, just very busy," Connie replied. "Hey, I was wondering if you could bring a dish of that wonderful peach cobbler you made. I would love to serve it for dessert at the R & R Tuesday night."

"Sure. No problem. How many should I plan for?" Alison asked. She could almost see Connie counting now, bobbing her head as she visualized the expected crowd.

"Oh...make enough for 30. Is that okay?" Connie asked.

"Fine. Do you need any help setting up at the Community Hall?" Alison asked.

"Oh, I forgot to tell you...we aren't having it there. We're having it in my backyard." There was silence on the line. Connie anticipated a "why" coming from Alison, so she simply explained, "Well, I'm planning on driving over to Fremont on Wednesday morning with all those chairs, tables, and boxes that are stored in my garage. I have to pull them out and reorganize the area. So I figure since I have them out, I may as well use them. Then I can just load my car up straight from my backyard. It seemed easier than taking everything over to the Community Hall and bringing it back again," she reasoned. "Will you come?"

"Tuesday evening?" Alison questioned.

"No dear, over to Fremont...on Wednesday. Marge said she would go with me, but she may not want to go after I tell everyone that I'm stepping down as event chairperson," Connie said.

Alison dreaded the thought of seeing those people over in the Fremont office of the National Cancer Association again, especially the blue slug.

"Is it okay if I pass on that one? I have a deadline that I'm behind on...I'm sorry, Connie." Alison didn't want to lie: Her work was, indeed, in need of attention. And besides, if Marge decides to go, she could help with the unloading if there was no staff from the office to help. Connie wouldn't be by herself.

"Hey, no problem. I'm really hoping Marge decides to go with me, it'll give us time alone to talk—time for the private apology I want to give to her as one of my committee chairpersons. This will work out fine. So I'll see you and a peach cobbler on Tuesday at 5 p.m.?"

You got it!" Alison said, smiling, and hung up the phone. Since it was Sunday night, it was her usual time to phone friends back East and make the compulsory call to the family that were usually never returned. No one was home as usual. She left a brief message, saying everything was fine and she was sorry the family couldn't make it out for a visit. Then there was Rick; she enjoyed her calls to him, but she was glad when Gracie, his wife—whom Alison really liked—answered the phone.

"Hi, Gracie!" Alison said. "How are the boys?" Rick and Gracie's two boys were both in high school. The oldest was a senior and scheduled to graduate this year.

"Just fine, thanks for asking," Gracie replied. She was a wonderful mother and came from a big family. She understood the brother-sister relationship that Alison and Rick shared and was not threatened by it. When Jack was alive, the two couples had enjoyed backyard barbeques and ball games together. Gracie understood the importance of Rick's work, and that made Alison feel closer to Gracie than to her own sister.

"Rick is at the office...."

"On a Sunday?" Alison interrupted.

"Yes, and it's for a good reason. They have had a huge breakthrough on one of the drugs Rick's team was working on. The whole team will be presenting the findings to the FDA at a meeting tomorrow. I'm sure he'll tell you all about," Gracie said enthusiastically. At that moment, Alison remembered the excitement she used to feel when a discovery at the lab was made. She missed being a part of it...and for a brief instant, she was a bit jealous of Rick.

"Well, I'm not going to bother him there…please tell him that everything's fine here. I'll call him at the office on Wednesday. You know you're all invited to visit…the boys would love rafting and fishing. Think about it for next summer, will you, Gracie?" Alison truly missed her surrogate family. They were such a comfort after Jack's death.

"It does sound wonderful, Alison, but with football and baseball camp year round, we just can't get away. Please keep the invitation open! Once the boys go away to school, it may be just Rick and me," Gracie replied.

"That would be wonderful. The two of you are welcome anytime," Alison said and meant every word sincerely. "Take care of the boys…all three of them," Alison said with a chuckle.

"Thanks for calling," Gracie said, then hung up.

"Oh, well," Alison thought to herself. "Now I have to answer the e-mails I've been trying to avoid." An hour passed, then Alison turned off the computer, checked all the doors in the house—a habit she had developed living on the East Coast all her life—and said good-night to Dinah. Turning off the lights, she went upstairs.

Chapter Twenty-four

Tuesday morning, the sky was gray with clouds forming over the foothills. Alison was readying Dinah for their usual walk down the bike path to the river, then around the park and back. Noticing the gray skies, she grabbed a sweater before leaving the house. The morning had a cold, crisp chill in the air that reminded Alison that summer was leaving and fall was approaching. This morning, she still wore a pair of hiking shorts, but she was glad she had grabbed the sweater.

The leaves on the cottonwood trees down by the river had lost their vibrant green color but still weren't ready to turn to radiant yellow. Fall had always been Alison's favorite season. The school buses, the crossing signs, and even the yellow stripes painted down the streets all shared the same rich yellow hue. Then, later on, there were the leaves that turned bright yellow and collected in the streets, swirling in the autumn breeze. She remembered how that yellow matched the rain boots and slickers on the children who would wait at the corner for the school crossing guard. Fall had always been a colorful, cheerful time of the year. These were the good memories of autumn that Alison still kept with her.

But now it was the first week in September. For Alison, new melancholy memories had replaced past happy childhood ones. Now with fall came reminders of loss—*her* loss. Next week, on the eleventh, would be the anniversary of Jack's death. Alison would put out the American flag in front of her house, visit her church, and say a silent prayer for Jack, as she had done for the past five years. Since that infamous September morning, Alison had always joined other families gathering at the center. People would come together, holding hands and offering a hug and a tear, feeling the common loss of their loved ones. Together, they would share and try to understand it. But this time would be different; this time, she couldn't drive over the bridge and visit the memorial. This time, she would be remembering Jack far away from the place where he died. His body was one of those they never found—she only had pictures and her memories as keepsakes of their love. Here in Rosemont, there was no one to share her grief. She was alone in this small town; there would be no memorial services and no crowds. She wasn't looking forward to next week.

Alison knew that staying busy kept her mind off such things, and now she tried to distract herself with a faster pace as she walked back home. Her fast stride reminded her of March at Night, and then it struck her: "That's the same emotional cord...!" Now she understood: It was the *importance* of the gathering, the walking hand in hand—it was *so important* not to ever forget the ones you love.

"Most of the people who came to the fundraiser came to share their grief, like I want to share my grief for Jack on September eleventh," Alison thought. For all her analytical ability, it had taken her this long to understand and realize how important sharing was—why the human spirit needs it and how the tears and hugs were an expression of that connection. It now seemed so obvious to her. How could she have overlooked the emotional element?

"But still...how can these folks continue with an event that drains the community of resources so badly needed right here—in their own community?" She remembered her walk around the track and her discussion with Janet. After what she'd heard from her about Connie, she knew Connie could handle that delicate balance between people's emotions and their egos. She had confidence that Connie could tell her many friends in this community the truth without insulting their motivation.

Later that day, Alison helped set up the tables and chairs on the lawn in Connie's backyard. Connie had some songs from the '70s playing in the house and, with the windows open, Alison could hear them faintly. The two women mostly worked in silence. Connie didn't use the aqua-colored tablecloths that were packed away in the NCA boxes. Nor were there any balloons or party favors scattered on each table. Instead, she had small mason jars with bunches of daisies in the center of each table. Alison then learned that daisies were Connie's favorite flower.

"Yup, they always seem to me to be such a happy flower, radiating out from the yellow center smiley face through each little white petal," Connie said as she arranged a bunch of them in a glass mason jar. "And they grow anywhere. I like that, too. Every place needs some happiness—especially this afternoon. Boy, will these people need some happiness!" she added as an afterthought.

Connie had assigned some of the women, who didn't work outside the home, a dish to bring to the barbeque. Besides the hamburgers and hot dogs, there would be a macaroni salad, potato salad, and local corn-on-the-cob served to the expected 30 people. She put up the badminton net and got out four rackets, hopefully offering some distractions for the squad leaders not reporting for any committee review meeting. An old boom box was moved onto the small patio off the kitchen. Connie had a big red tub, the kind Alison saw at Murdock's feed store for livestock, and was filling it with ice. Cans of Coke and Diet Pepsi were then scattered on top.

Deception in a Small Town

People started arriving at 4 o'clock and claimed their seats at one of the tables. Some were saving places for friends they knew were coming. Connie was busy in the kitchen, preparing the buns and burgers. Alison arranged the serving table with white paper plates and plastic spoons in the same sequence Connie had used at the Recruitment Rally. Connie peeked out of the kitchen to inspect, smiling at Alison and giving her an "okay" sign with her left hand.

The boom box was blasting out Johnny Lee's "Lookin' for Love" when Connie called "Chow's on!" from the patio. She banged on the back of a steel pot with a wooden spoon to attract everyone's attention. Alison had to giggle to herself…she really appreciated Connie's sense of humor. Connie caught Alison's look and gave her a wink.

People started getting up from their tables and the chow line formed. The smell and smoke from the charcoal grill filled the afternoon air, swirling in every direction. The breeze shifted the sounds of laughter, music, and the sizzle of meat cooking back and forth in the backyard. Alison watched everyone, offering a smile to those she recognized. While the people waited, paper plates in hand, they began to tap the toes of their boots on the patio concrete in time to the music. Alison found an empty place at one of the far tables and sat down, smiling to herself; she was glad she had moved to this community and glad the weather had cooperated with the barbeque.

❧ Chapter Twenty-five ❧

An hour later, people were relaxed and full. The afternoon breeze continued, preventing any real game of badminton, but most didn't seem to mind. They were just glad to gather and chat at the tables. Voices and laugher came from one table, then from the other.

Once the tables had been cleared, the music coming from the boom box stopped playing. Connie was standing at the kitchen door and, again, started banging the metal pot with the wooden spoon.

"Folks, I have an announcement…please gather around!" Connie banged on her pot one more time. The laughter stopped and everyone turned around to face her. She was now standing on a wooden box placed on the patio.

"First, I want to thank everyone for coming. It has really been my pleasure to host this R & R party. You all have done a tremendous job at the event this year, and please know that this afternoon doesn't even come close to the thanks you deserve for all your hard work and the money you raised." The backyard filled with hoots, hollers, and applause. "Yes, you all deserve a round of applause." Connie started clapping, looking into the crowd of smiling faces—faces of people she knew and loved. "You all know how great you did this year, and that's yours forever." The applause began again and then, seeing the serious look on Connie's face, it stopped.

Connie waited until the group was quiet, then she spoke again. "I have recently learned things about the National Cancer Association that will not allow me, in good conscience, to continue as your National Cancer Association event chair next year…or in any future year…." The crowd went completely silent. "This was my decision, and please know that no one asked me to step down, and no one forced me to, either—it is my choice." There were a few whispers from the crowd, but Connie waited until the information had settled.

"What I have learned…is what I want to share with you—so then you can make your own decisions about the future of this event in our community.

"Who has heard of the Brooks Trust?" Connie bluntly threw the question out to the crowd. People looked at each other, wondering what this was all about.

"Well, I hadn't heard of it either until a few weeks ago. I learned that 20 years ago, the National Cancer Association here in Colorado was endowed with a trust fund—the Brooks Trust—of over three million dollars." People were looking puzzled.

"The Colorado Division of the NCA had legal rights to spend the three million dollars as they saw fit. Now, we all know what their mission statement is, and we all know that for the past four years, we've been asking them for help here in rural Colorado. But, even knowing the good they could do with this money from the Trust, they decided to do nothing with the three million dollars. Then 12 years ago, the executives of the NCA told the people of Colorado that the organization was keeping the money…keeping it to ensure the salaries of the executives and staff." There was buzzing and whispers coming from the crowd.

"How many of us have lost loved ones to cancer over those 12 years?" Connie asked those seated. "Well, I have...and Marge...and Janet...."

"What's this all about...!?" came a man's angry voice from the crowd. "I don't remember reading about that in the paper!"

"Hear me out.... I know, I didn't remember hearing or reading about it, either," Connie offered. "But we all remember the winter of '93, when none of us could get over the passes...and you, George, you lost ten head of cattle that winter."

"You're right about that, Connie," George responded.

"I doubt if any of us were paying much attention to a position statement that came out of the Denver courts that winter."

Connie, scanning the group, found Sally in the crowd. "Sally, when did your mother die of cancer?" she asked, looking directly at Sally.

"Ten years ago...this was her tenth year anniversary," Sally answered, wanting everyone else to hear as well.

"I remember it was late-term colon cancer, wasn't it?" Connie asked.

"Yes," Sally replied. "You *do* remember," she said in surprise.

"And she suffered for over a year and a half, isn't that right?"

"Yes...it was very hard on the whole family—especially Dad. She was only 51 years old."

"Remember how your family was told that if she had been screened earlier and the cancer detected sooner, that her chances would have been better?" Connie asked rhetorically.

"Yes."

"The money that was there in the National Cancer Association's bank account from the Brooks Trust could have covered her screening for colon cancer, as it could have for others who live in rural communities like ours, but the NCA didn't help—

they did nothing. With their money, we could have had our Cancer Center ten years earlier. Or they could have bought our community hospital two new colonoscopy machines and offered screenings for residents over the age of 50, but they didn't—they chose to keep the money, all that time taking donor dollars from small communities like ours."

"Marge, when was Frank finally diagnosed with end-stage prostate cancer?" Connie asked, finding Marge at the front table.

"1998—you know…with him farming most of the year up on Shoefly Flats, he didn't come into town too often," Marge said defensively, as if it was Frank's fault.

"What if we had a mobile X-ray machine and prostate screening tests that could visit the communities at that end of the county? The National Cancer Association had the money to purchase one for our county and the next one over, yet they chose to keep the money.

"How many of our loved ones…my John included…would be alive today if the National Cancer Association had kept their promise?" There were low whispers from the gathering.

"At the start of this year's event, we were all asked to sign a contract with the National Cancer Association—a pledge to work hard and volunteer our time and effort in raising funds for their organization. When I signed that contract, as most of you did, I trusted the National Cancer Association to spend the money wisely, and in this community's best interests. Now, after four years of asking our small community for money, I learn that the whole time, they have been holding the purse strings to over three million dollars—dollars that could have saved lives. They have lied to me for four years and they have deceived you, too. The organization has broken the contract that I signed. My disappointment in them is overwhelming. I will never trust them… I *can't* trust them."

"What about cancer research?" came a voice from the crowd.

"That's also a disappointing fact. We were all led to believe that our money goes to cancer research; whenever the NCA staff was asked how much of our dollars go to cancer research, we were never given a straight answer. Well, I've learned that it is only 15%!" Connie was angry but calm, waiting for the information to slowly sink in.

"You're telling me that for every dollar we've raised, only 15 cents has gone back to cancer research? They will never find a cure that way!" Libby piped up.

"That should be illegal…misrepresentation, or something…," someone said.

"It was pointed out to me that they are doing nothing illegal; we trusted them and donated freely—that's not illegal. It was also pointed out to me that having an affair with another man's wife is not illegal. But it sure is immoral and unethical by most people's standards—and especially mine! I see it the same way. They cheated on me. They have lost my trust, because they signed that contract, too, and when they cheated and lied to me, they broke that contract. Trust is what most contracts are based on, and there can be no trust for me with a cheatin' spouse or an unethical organization. I'm glad I know the truth, and now you all do, too. I think of John and what he would want me to do. I know by stepping down, I'm not only doing the right thing, but it would've been what he would've wanted, too."

Alison, listening to Connie, was moved by her very personal and sincere argument. She was convincingly honest. "Jack would have liked Connie's tenacity," Alison thought to herself.

"What I plan to do," Connie continued, "is to volunteer for our local organizations that help those families who have a loved one suffering from cancer. I will make sure that my efforts are kept right here—for the people of our community. The past is the past, and I can't do anything about it. What I can do starts now, from this point forward, and I intend to spend my time volunteering for our local nonprofits. You are all welcome to join me—we do have fun together, don't we? And it would be my privilege to work with any of you in the future."

Alison began to applaud, slowly at first until others joined in. As they did, the applause grew and people started standing. Alison's eyes began to well up with tears.

Then, from somewhere in the group came an angry woman's voice, "What about us? So you're leavin' us just holdin' the bag?" The applause stopped and the group was again quiet. "I drive two hours to meet with friends and March at Night. I've been doin' it since you started the whole thing. My Davie is buried here in Rosemont. He died of cancer, too. I come over, have some BBQ, and March at Night with my friends. Then in the morning I visit Davie's grave…. It's been that way since you started me marching. How're ya gonna replace that?" Alison watched Connie's reaction. It seemed this woman was familiar to Connie. By the look of abandonment on many of the faces, she could see the question was in many of their hearts, too.

"Listen, you know I love this community event as much as you all do, and that was the part I had a tough time with—ya know, letting go of that. But we're the ones doing all the work each year, so let's just keep doing it! We can have the high school athletic field, the BBQ, the music, and the costumes…. We can have the fundraising, but the money will stay *here* in Rosemont and go to the Cancer Center for diagnostic equipment and helping those families suffering. We don't have to stop. Like I said—I'm not going to!"

"Okay," the woman countered, "but what about the National Cancer Association? Won't they be upset?"

"They have their three million dollars…they don't need any more of mine!" Connie said emphatically. "What about you?"

The woman didn't reply.

"Tomorrow, I'll be going over to Fremont with NCA property and supplies. If any of the committee chairs have any items belonging to that organization, and you do not intend to use them in the future, please have them here in front of my garage by 9 a.m. Otherwise, you will have to answer to the NCA yourselves. Again, thank you all for coming!"

Connie got off her soap box and went over to the boom box. The music started playing Jimmy Lee's "Cherokee Fiddle."

Some of the women from the committees, like Sally and Libby, went up to Connie, offering hugs and thanks. Alison stayed at the back of the crowd, watching the group. Most were quietly cleaning up the backyard, folding chairs and tables. Alison worked until seven, then walked into the kitchen to say goodnight to Connie.

"Hey, what you did was very difficult. You handled it very well," Alison said. She sat down at Connie's kitchen table that was piled with chafing dishes and jars of condiments.

"Personally, it wasn't the easiest thing for me to mentally work through—the realization that for four years, those people from the NCA have used my emotions to deceive me and this community. After what I learned, I really didn't have much choice," Connie said. "I knew John would be okay with it, too."

"How do the think most people will take it?"

"I'm not sure…. I could tell some were really mad about all the money they've given in the past, and others are sad and upset because they just liked coming to the event. Others will have a hard time accepting the fact that such a large national organization deceived our community.

"And some people in town won't even care what the truth is. They would follow the devil to hell if it made them feel better or fed their egos," Connie said. "Don't worry about what those people think, Alison….

Deception in a Small Town

"Most folks in this town have to come to their own conclusions to be convinced...but sometimes they have to be shown the way, like you showed me," she went on. "Like you said, it's all about choices. Well, we'll see tomorrow, won't we...we'll see what's left on my driveway to take over to Fremont," Connie said with a smile.

◈ Chapter Twenty-six ◈

The next day Connie didn't call, much to Alison's relief. It meant that Marge had decided to drive with her over to Fremont. It was a crisp, clear morning. Alison, with Dinah on her leash, walked the shorter route. She could feel the change in the weather. She knew the coming snows would force her into the office, so she decided to spend the rest of this lovely autumn morning outdoors, cleaning up the backyard. The flowers on the hollyhocks had turned to dried paper petals and the hummingbirds had stopped coming around, so Alison took the feeders down. The cottonwoods had only a few clusters of yellow leaves, but soon the trees would be the color of the school buses and children's rain boots Dinah kept Alison company, playing with a pinecone that was blown down from a neighboring tree. Alison was anxious to hear the outcome of Connie's visit to Fremont, so she needed to stay busy until her return.

At 3:30, Alison's phone rang. It was Connie.

"Tell me all about it!" Alison said expectantly. "How did it go…who was there? Did Marge go with you?"

"Why don't you meet me outside on my porch? We can sit and I'll tell you what happened," Connie said. Alison welcomed the opportunity to hear every detail.

Connie had set out a plate of gingersnaps, two tall glasses, and a pitcher of iced tea. "Hey there," she said as Alison came out on the back porch. "I've had a long day, so go easy on me with the questions, Alison," Connie pleaded. "Let me start at the beginning.

"I went out this morning to find a lot of boxes sitting in my driveway. I dreaded that all night, so you can image my relief to see them from the facility committee—that was Bert's from the high school. You remember—you met him," Connie said.

"Yes, of course—go on," Alison prodded.

"There were boxes from the PR committee, the financial committee, and the food and beverage committees. Seems most of the committee chairs turned in their event materials. I took it as confirmation that some of the volunteers would not be participating next year. Marge was very reserved when she came over—I knew her feelings were hurt, and I respect that," Connie said. "We have known each other for 30 years.

"Well, because most everything was packed the night before, we were able to finish loading the car by 9:30. Marge and I talked the whole way over. At first, she was upset that I didn't tell her I was stepping down before the R & R. But when I explained to her it had nothing to do with trust, and that it was just the most fair approach I could take towards the entire committee, she eventually forgave me—but only after a half-hour of driving." Connie said.

"The rest of the drive, I explained to her how I wanted to handle the situation in Fremont," Connie chuckled, then took a gulp of iced tea.

"When we arrived at the Fremont office, I went upstairs to get a small trolley to move all the boxes. Maxine was at her desk."

"So *that's* the blue slug's name," Alison thought.

"She told me that the staff was having a very important meeting and that I wouldn't be allowed to speak with any of them, but that I could leave the message with her. I told her we would wait.

"She is the most obnoxious woman I have ever met," Connie added. "After our second trip upstairs with boxes, she began questioning us like the Gestapo. She wanted to know why all the event boxes and banners were being brought back. Marge just told her that she would find out from a staff member…but not her! Marge was great!" Connie smiled and popped a gingersnap into her mouth.

"Then Maxine became very arrogant and told us we couldn't leave everything in her office, and that I was responsible for all of it because I was the event chair for the Rosemont fundraiser. She kept saying, 'Don't argue with me—I'm with the National Cancer Association.' Blah blah blah….

"Well, you must have learned by now, Alison, that I like to have fun with folks, and I wanted to make Maxine seem insignificant. After four years of dealing with that smug woman, I know it's what she hates the most. So, I politely told her that she would find out soon enough, and that everything was going upstairs…and if she didn't take it into her office, we would leave it in the hallway and call the building manager and fire department, informing them of a fire hazard outside the National Cancer Association's office. I politely smiled again and told her there wasn't much more to bring up…so I lied," Connie said with a false innocence.

"What did she say?" Alison asked.

"Nothing; she just looked nervous. I think she really thought we *would* call the fire department. Marge and I politely smiled and said we would wait in her office until the staff meeting was over. That frustrated her even more—and that made it all worth it!

"Anyway, Marge and I started stacking up all the boxes until they were three high and four deep—it took us five trips to the SUV. When we finished, there were rolls of banners and flags and plastic storage bins everywhere. Well, it looked like the contents of my garage had been dropped into the front office of the NCA. I have to tell you, Alison, it gave me such pleasure to see the annoyed look on that nasty woman's face." Connie seemed amused as she told the story.

"Then, after Marge and I had been sitting, waiting for the meeting to be over, Maxine got up to use the women's room. Maxine, being as big as she is, had a hard time getting around the stacked boxes or squeezing between them. She couldn't get from her desk to the office door," Connie started laughing. "I will confess—but only to you, Alison—that we intentionally arranged the boxes so both Marge and I could squeeze by, but Maxine would have a tough time getting around them. You should have seen it; it was hilarious! We were just sitting in the front office watching, pretending to read a magazine, and we couldn't help giggling like schoolgirls, aware of Maxine's situation." Connie took a gulp of iced tea and let out a chuckle as she replayed the scene in her mind.

"When Maxine realized she was the joke, her face got so red and sweaty.... You know—you've seen her get agitated! Well, she didn't know what to do. She couldn't squeeze between the boxes to the hallway and she wouldn't move them. So, she huffed and puffed down the other hallway to the conference room, knocked on the door, and went inside. From the front office, we could hear loud voices and shouting coming from inside the conference room.

"Then the door opened, and Juanita Montoya slithered out into the hall. She was wearing her latest outfit...black pants and tunic," Connie sarcastically said. "The queen was suspiciously pleasant and invited me and Marge into the conference room."

"Oh dear...did you go in? Or did you tell her off, right there in the hallway?" Alison piped in.

"Who's telling this story?" Connie countered. "You will never believe what they told me."

"*They?*" Alison excitedly fired back.

"Well, of course! You can't have a meeting by yourself! Be patient, I'm getting to that," Connie smiled like the Cheshire cat.

"Marge took my lead, and we followed her into the conference room. Maxine, who was standing by the door, left and closed it behind her. Marge and I were offered seats around the conference table. Mitch Cutter was there, of course, and Marcia Harris; that short stocky fellow that follows Juanita everywhere was there. You remember—he's the one that accused you of taking the cash box," Connie said.

"Oh, yes—how could I forget him," Alison responded.

"And there were two other people who I haven't seen before…a man and a woman. They were very well dressed," Connie said, remembering the scene.

"After we sat down, Juanita stood at the front of the room and started telling everyone what a wonderful person I was; that I was the hardest working volunteer and the best event chairperson their organization ever had, and how reliable I was. Marge and I looked at each other: We couldn't believe what we were hearing.

"She told everyone how important I was in the community and how much the NCA appreciated me; how it was people like me who would help the NCA find the future cure for cancer. And then she said how the entire organization is looking forward to working with me next year.

"Alison, it was disgusting. It was so saccharine sweet, oozing with insincerity; it was two-faced and hypocritical. I sat there wondering why she was saying all those things…for whose benefit? Was it for the two visitors at the table or for me?"

"Who were the others?" Alison asked.

"Well, I was never introduced, but by the way they were treating them, I think they must have been big shots…probably Juanita's bosses. My only other clue to who they were was—on one of our trips to the parking lot—I noticed three Cadillac Escalades all parked in a row. So, being the nosy person I am—and noticing only Marge and I were in the parking lot—I peeked in the window and saw a large binder on the passenger seat in the front.... It had the National Cancer Association logo on it, and there were papers all over the floor of the car, and the back seat was full of fly-fishing equipment. There was a letter on the dashboard of one of the Escalades addressed to the Regional Vice President.

"You'd make a great investigator!" Alison said.

"Well, that's what made me think they were big shots from NCA headquarters. Besides that, while Juanita spoke, everyone in the room was bobbing their heads in agreement with drugged-looking grins on their faces—obedient mindless clones! I thought I'd stepped into the Twilight Zone...I was just waiting for Rod Serling to walk through the door into the room. It was surreal!" Connie said with a laugh.

"Almost like stepping through the looking glass!" Alison said in return.

"Yeah! I was so glad Marge was with me, mostly for moral support."

"What did Marge do?" Alison asked, riveted by the story.

"Not much. She poked me once under the table and gave me a couple of looks when we heard the blatant lies. It was like we were the only ones on the *Titanic* who knew the ship was sinking. The others were playing in the band or rearranging the deck chairs. The whole thing was so absurd, but no one besides Marge and me seemed to notice. The people in the room who knew she was spouting exaggerations about our event said nothing—they just smiled.

"I couldn't wait for my opportunity to tell them all that was on my mind. Actually, her remarks only reinforced my convictions," Connie added. "The more I listened to her lie about our event—how we made goal and how we had a model event committee, always following the best practice rules…all that drivel—I just got madder and madder.

"Then I thought to myself, if that speech was for my benefit, did she really think I was so stupid and my ego so important to me that I would buy into these false compliments? Alison, I was insulted and embarrassed for this delusional woman. I couldn't think why she was being so deceitful."

"If she sensed you were quitting, then that would explain her behavior," Alison interjected.

"If that was true, did she think those insincere compliments would win me back?" Connie asked rhetorically. Alison sensed Connie was holding something back, as if she already had the answer.

Taking a sip of tea, Alison said, "I don't really know. Perhaps it was for the benefit of the visitors. If they were her bosses, then it would look really bad for her if you quit in front of them," she added thoughtfully. She looked over at Connie and saw a smile come over her friend's face.

"Well…," Connie said, grinning ear to ear, "that's exactly what I did!"

"What!?" Alison said. Then, seeing the satisfied look of victory on Connie's face, she started laughing hysterically, not able to speak. Finally, she was able to control herself enough to say, "Good for you, Connie—bravo!" Connie joined in the laughter. Alison continued, "What did you say? Tell me, tell me, how you did it!

"Well, when that awful woman finished, she began clapping for me, then the others joined in. That's when I stood up—they probably thought I was standing to take a humble and thankful bow—but instead, I walked to the front of the room. "I stood there at the head of the table until the clapping stopped, then I told them that I had signed a contract with the

Deception in a Small Town

National Cancer Association to volunteer for the organization as the chairperson of the Rosemont event. And, while it was merely a symbolic gesture—not a legal document—it still was my promise to their organization. I told them that for four years I have honored that promise. This year, like the past three years, their organization, represented by their staff and management, has told our community, by way of promises and symbolic contracts, that we will get services and programs from the NCA. 'That *is* your mission statement, isn't it?' I asked. I put the question out there to them. The well-dressed man started glaring at Juanita. Then I told them, 'We're still waiting for you to fulfill your end of the contract.'

"I told them that we have also learned that during those four years, the Colorado Division of the National Cancer Association has had over three million dollars from the Brooks Trust that they chose not to spend—not even towards their mission statement. And that learning this made me feel used and deceived. I told them that I volunteered for personal reasons and I am quitting for personal reasons. That the National Cancer Association was unethical in hidding this information about the Brooks Trust, all the time asking our small community for donations. I can never support any organization, especially a nonprofit one, whose actions are defined by such hypocrisy."

"That's great, Connie," Alison encouraged.

Connie smiled and continued, "Yeah, I thought so, too. But it gets better....

"At that point, the woman I didn't know interrupted me and said that the Brooks Trust was out of their hands.... But I cut off her excuse-making and said, 'I understand there were no laws broken, and I'm sure you have a number of law firms on retainer.' I told them that I also knew that, as a corporation, they have bonuses, pension plans, and investments in property and assets...and that it seemed to me that their first priority was the corporation's financial strength, and not their mission statement. Their managers' goals and budget seem to be more important than a cure for cancer, and that a cure for cancer would be bad for business!"

"Did you really?" Alison said.

"Yup, and boy did that shut her up. She just sat there and glared at Juanita Montoya, who was avoiding looking at her."

"Then Mitch piped in and asked, 'What ya gonna do?' Before I could say anything, Juanita Montoya got up and—showing her true colors—called me a naïve, ungrateful, and stupid woman. Her face was beet red. Then the well-dressed man stood and told her to be quiet and sit down. He must have been her boss, because she immediately sat down—she was fuming. He apologized to Marge and me. Then he told Juanita that her display was uncalled for, and that this was a private matter that should have been handled one-on-one with the volunteer…that this division was her responsibility, and he would make sure that this incident would appear on her performance record; that she was responsible for any loss of revenue or bad publicity.

"Then she started pointing her finger at Mitch, who was down the table, and said it was his fault for letting it go so far and letting that 'outsider' into the event before she was checked out. I think she was talking about you, Alison! You're the only new person who's helped with this year's event. Anyway, she said 'heads would roll,' referring to Mitch's, of course. Mitch turned to Marcia and said that it was her fault, 'cause she was always so pushy, and then blamed her for all the problems and shortfalls in what he referred to as 'revenue,' saying it was her job as Financial Development Director. Can you imagine? Our donations are perceived as *their* revenue! Marcia seemed very indignant and defensive. She looked over and pointed to Juanita…evidently Marcia answers to her," Connie added. "I never really cared to learn the food chain in that organization, but it sure seemed like a feeding frenzy in that conference room. She started accusing Juanita of giving her impossible goals and told the well-dressed man that Juanita didn't care how it got done, it was 'Just do it!'

"You were right, Alison—everything was about the money! It's always been about the money. They were more dysfunctional than any fifth grade class I ever had in my 20 years of teaching! The well-dressed man just watched the display, as though he was keeping a mental scorecard on each of them," Connie reflected. "They continued the finger-pointing—no one said anything to us. It was like we had disappeared," Connie said. "So I motioned to Marge, who got up from her chair, and we left them in the conference room—still arguing."

"Well, good for you, Connie. I'm proud of you!" Alison praised her friend. Connie continued to beam with satisfaction as she mentally played back the scene. Alison sat back in her porch chair, then—looking over at Connie—asked, "Do you think what you said will change anything?"

"As far as what?" Connie countered. Then, realizing the meaning, replied, "Oh yes, it will change what we do here in Rosemont...that's for sure!" she said emphatically.

"No, I mean about the organization," Alison directed.

"Probably not...oh, I suppose a few staff members will be blamed and have to quit, or even be fired—the staff turnover in that organization is very high—but in general, I don't think much will change. Our community won't get any more services...and they'll keep asking for our money."

"You're probably right about that," Alison answered, thinking back on Professor Bennett's book. "Their organization is national, with too many ties to Federal agencies. If anything changes, it will have to come community-by-community across the country. It's just a shame that people in other small rural towns don't take it upon themselves—like you've decided to here in Rosemont—and start their own 501-C3 nonprofit organizations to help each other," Alison said. "I guess we're pretty lucky to have our own here."

"Yup, I think so, too. As a matter of fact, Marge and I talked about it the whole way back from Fremont. She agreed that many people just enjoyed getting together for what they thought was a good cause. So instead of planning for next year's March at Night, we're going to have a fundraiser for Bosom Buddies and the local Hospice."

"Oh, you are so clever," Alison told her friend.

"We already have the meeting schedule set through this fall and into winter, but we're going to set our fundraising goals for a mobile X-ray machine or something the Cancer Center really needs. It may take us two years, but at least the folks will know what we're saving for and where the money is being spent. Marge and I are going to ask everyone from last year's committee to join us. We'll have food and music—a real community celebration! Best of all, Marge promised to be in charge!" Connie added enthusiastically. Alison was amazed at their "can-do" attitude.

"The moment we got back into Rosemont, Marge called Clare over at the Cancer Center, and then went over to see her. From their short phone conversation, Marge thinks Clare will be behind it 100%."

"It all sounds wonderful…can I help?" Alison asked.

"Of course! As a matter of fact, you already have," Connie smiled. "You've given me the courage to know that my love for John will never go away, and the guilt and sorrow I still harbor over his passing cannot be replaced by volunteer busyness for an organization with a big name and no ethics.

"You were bullied by those people from the National Cancer Association, and everyone at the event saw it, too. They saw the same thing they've been putting up with for the past four years. You helped me show my friends and this community the truth—how this national nonprofit was bullying us in order to make their 'revenue' goal—more money!

"Thank you for all of that, Alison," Connie said, and meant it. The two women sat on the porch, sipping iced tea and nibbling on gingersnaps as the late afternoon sun filtered through the bare branches of the old cottonwoods.

Then a smile came over Connie face, and she said, "Ya know, I wasn't gonna say anything, but I'm just as bad at keeping a secret from a friend...." Alison looked over at Connie. "Ya wanna know what tipped it for me?"

"Sure," Alison said, taking a bite of gingersnap.

"It was when they all started marching across the field to you that night when they accused you of stealing the cash box. I knew what was coming," Connie said sheepishly.

"You what? You *knew* they would accuse me of stealing, and you just let them?" Alison asked, not knowing whether to be mad or hurt.

"Kinda—I wasn't sure what the accusation would be, but I knew you were in their cross-hairs—they were out to get you. So I had to wait; I had to let it play out. I knew how Juanita's staff would react," Connie said. "People had to come to their own conclusions to be convinced—they had to be shown the same way that I was shown. They had to see it for themselves. So I waited...."

"Why?" Alison countered suspiciously.

"To expose their true agenda! By then, I was convinced they didn't care about us or their own mission statement, but I had to show everyone else on the field that night that those people didn't care about the volunteers, or a cure, or hope—it was just about the money!" Connie said triumphantly.

"Everyone on the field that night saw the way you were treated. The community had to see for themselves how they bullied a volunteer for money."

"You *used* me?" Alison said incredulously.

"Sort of...but it was for a good cause!" Connie replied. Alison finally chuckled, appreciating the cynical humor. "And it worked!" Connie said, trying to change the focus.

"Well, I *hope* it worked!" Alison said.

"I think most people will come to realize it and choose wisely, once we get our own community event going next year," Connie added.

"Remember when you asked me if you were any help. Oh boy, have you been a help!" Connie said to her friend. Alison said nothing, just smiled back.

"Thanks," Alison said, "glad I could be of service...I think...."

The two women began to laugh at the events of the summer, as they ate gingersnaps and drank iced tea on the back porch of a two-story clapboard home in a small town in rural Colorado. It was a late autumn afternoon, the sun just setting behind the homes. The storm clouds that had passed earlier were now in the evening sky, glowing pinks and reds in the twilight. The spring had turned to fall and Alison felt content in her new home... in her new town. The moment took Alison back to the first day she met Connie; two women in the corner of a backyard, talking over a shared white picket fence. She remembered the though she had that day, of a moment such as this, and now she was thinking, "Norman Rockwell should be painting this scene, too."

CPSIA information can be obtained at www.ICGtesting.com
230583LV00001B/16/P